Before the Storm

Before the Storm

A Steel & Thunder Prequel

DOMINIC N. ASHEN

4 Horsemen
Publications, Inc.

4 Horsemen
Publications, Inc.

4 Horsemen Publications, Inc.
1497 Main St. Suite 169
Dunedin, FL 34698
4horsemenpublications.com
info@4horsemenpublications.com

Cover Art by Oxford
Cover typography by Niki Tantillo
Typesetting by Autumn Skye
Edited by Tilda M. Cooke

Library of Congress Control Number: 2023932952

Paperback ISBN-13: 978-1-64450-884-8
Audiobook ISBN-13: 978-1-64450-887-9
Ebook ISBN-13: 978-1-64450-886-2

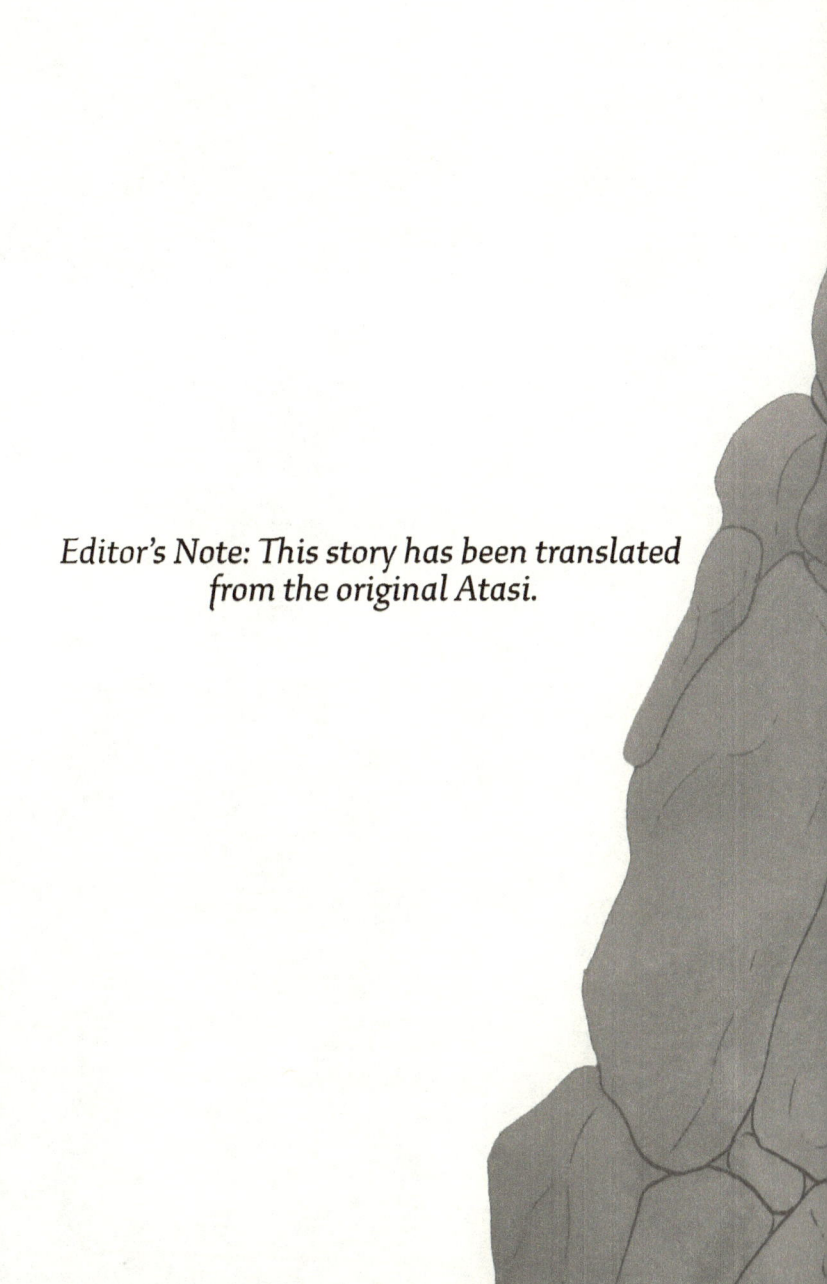

Editor's Note: This story has been translated from the original Atasi.

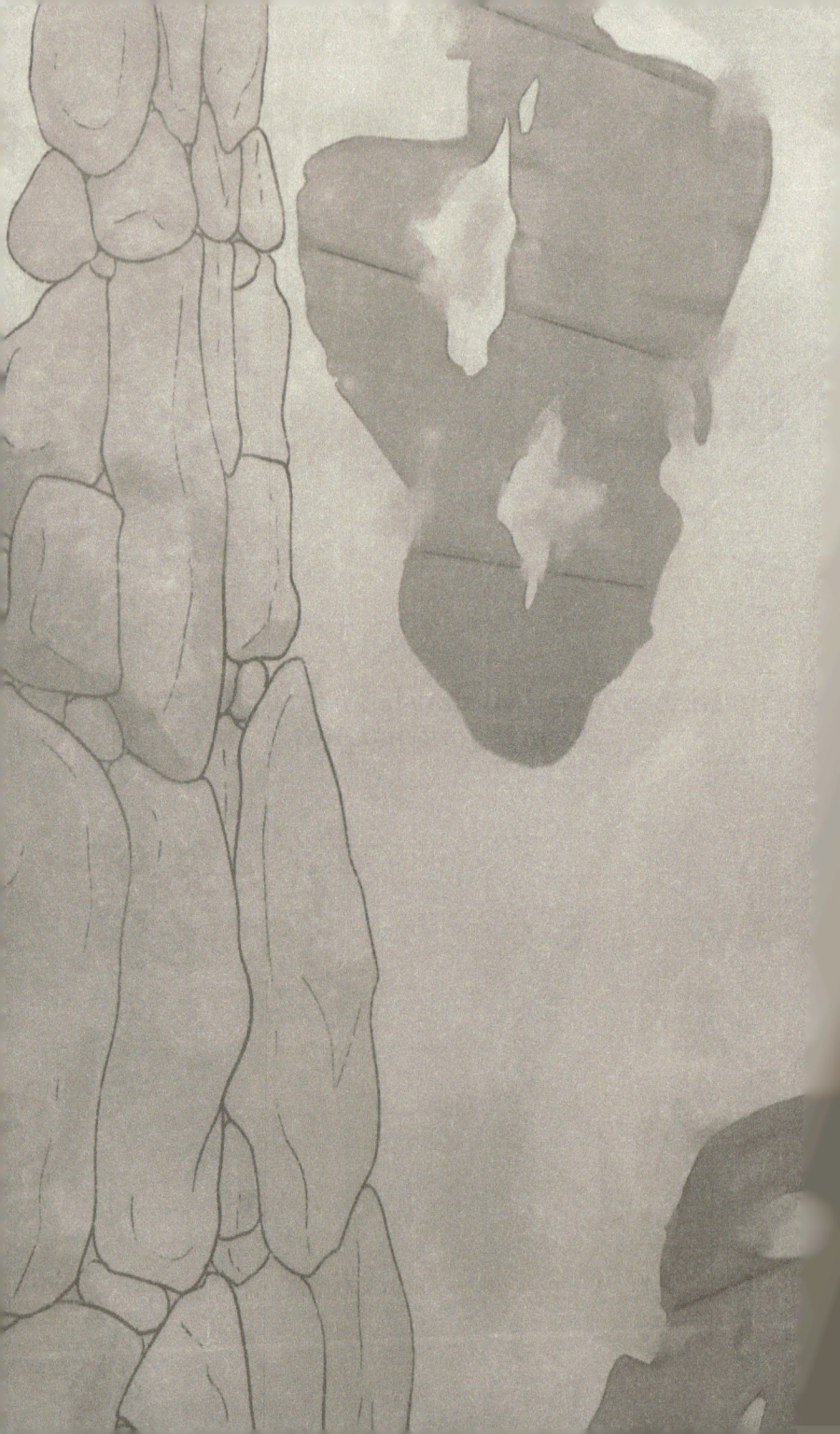

Table of Contents

Chapter 1

Orlun

"No staying up late."

"Yes, Orda," my son, Khazak, responds with a nod.

"Listen to your brother," I tell my daughter Ayla next. "Help him to watch Yogik when he gets up from his nap."

"Yes, Orda..." she answers much more reluctantly.

"Dinner is in the icebox." I kiss both on the forehead before releasing them and standing. "Sor'iya will be by to check on you in a few hours. What are you supposed to remember?"

"Not to open the door for anyone but her, you, or Ruda," they answer in unison.

"I love you both." I bend over to give them one last hug.

"Love you too, Orda."

"...Love you too."

"I expect everyone to be asleep by the time we return home." With one final look around my home, I nod my head and exit, shutting and locking the door behind me.

The late afternoon sun hangs in the sky when I step outside. Despite the relatively early hour, it has been an extremely long day, and it is only going to get longer. After I finished my shift at the ranger station, I rushed home to change and check on the children. I was barely there more than an hour before having to leave again, now heading for the militia headquarters where my husband Rurig is already working.

Our schedules are not normally quite this hectic. Of course things got busier after having children, but between the two of us, we've been able to handle things without too many problems. Other than my monthly week-long patrol shifts in the forest, my schedule does not change much—a benefit of being the man in charge. Rurig still works as a chef at The Iron Pan, the restaurant we opened together years ago, but he cut his hours back significantly after the children were born so he could stay home with them—something he was not very happy about.

Once Ayla and Khazak were old enough to start attending school, he could not wait to get back in the kitchen. Even after our youngest son, Yogik, was born, he told me he'd had enough of sitting around fussing after babies. He returned to the restaurant with Yogik in tow, setting up a small nursery, and later playroom, in his back office. From what I hear, my son is very popular with some of the servers.

Normally Rurig would be home in the early afternoon, before Khazak and Ayla return from school, and I would follow several hours later. But thanks to Warhunter and his so-called "rebellion," all of our evenings have been claimed for the near future. Instead of staying home with our children, we have been working with the defense militia every night.

We were both members when we were younger—which is actually how we met—but that was over a decade ago. Long in the tusks compared to the other recruits, neither of us is directly involved in any of the current battles.

Orlun

However, many of my men are, and as their captain, sitting on the sidelines is not an option—and unfortunately in the eyes of many others, that also goes for the captain's husband. So rather than fighting, we are putting our other skills to use: Rurig working in the mess hall, and me helping to train the new recruits.

This all started around a month ago when former-Councilman Kragor Warhunter announced that he would not be stepping down from his seat at the end of his term. Touting a belief that the strong should rule over the weak, he then declared his intent to violently depose the rest of the Tribal Council. Most of us saw this as nothing more than posturing until he made good on his threat, attacking and killing one of the other councilmembers and sending the city's government into chaos.

Perhaps the only thing more surprising than his attack was how quickly he was able to raise supporters. I would hardly call them an army, but they number enough for the militia to rally a full defense. Thankfully, most of the fighting has taken place outside of the city. After his initial attack, Warhunter and his troops were forced into the forest where they have been hiding in makeshift camps. They seem to have recruited several powerful spellcasters to his side as we have been having difficulty locating them—even with magic. Few battles have occurred within V'rok'sh Tah'lj's walls, and the ones that have we have managed to contain in one section of the city.

I arrive at militia headquarters after a twenty-minute walk, returning the salute given to me by the two guards at the front gate. It is as busy as it ever is these days with dozens of people with their own orders and expectations. Militia Captain Gibnil Burningmaw is already in the yard with a group of recruits. I need to get my equipment and join him, but first I am going to stop by the mess hall to greet my husband.

"Hello, Captain!" One of the troops stands and salutes me as I enter, causing most of the others in the mess hall to do the same. I return the salute, encouraging the man that greeted me and the others to return to their seats. The title really makes it seem like I do more around here than train.

"Oh, has the big strong Ranger Captain stopped by to see me?" Rurig exaggerates as I approach.

"No, just feeling a little peckish," I tease as he walks around the counter that separates the kitchen from the dining area, greeting me with a kiss.

"How are the kids?" he asks once we separate.

"Fine," I answer with a small smile. "I put Yogik down for a nap before I left."

"I hope he'll sleep most of the night," he responds with a sigh. Getting Yogik to sleep at all lately has been difficult.

You may be worried that we would leave our children home alone during a time such as this, but I can assure you, they are safe and sound. Not only is there a strict curfew in effect, but all the fighting has taken place far, far from our home. Our two older children are eight-year-old twins and very mature for their age; Khazak in particular is an extremely responsible boy. Rurig will see them off to school and ensure they have food prepared for the day, then leave for his shift at the mess hall once they are home. I see them next when I have finished work, and then in the evenings we have our elderly neighbor, Sor'iya Drakebloom, check in on them before it gets too late. I was happy when she accepted our request—the Ranger Captain asking for help might be seen as a weakness by some, especially right now, and I cannot afford for that to happen.

With my husband greeted, I leave the mess hall and retrieve my training equipment from the small office I share with some of the other officers. Then I join Captain Burningmaw on the field. The cadre we are training today are still fairly new, all having joined in the past month. Fighting in the name of protecting the city is seen as a great honor, so it is no surprise that the militia has received an influx of recruits since Warhunter's initial attack.

They have varying levels of skill, but working with new troops is something I am familiar with. I regularly sit in on and even participate in training sessions with new officers to the ranger force, which is why Burningmaw requested my presence. The two of us will demonstrate techniques on each other before having the recruits try for themselves.

We are still working on positioning with this particular group. I walk around them, all twenty facing Burningmaw as he runs them through a drill. I monitor their progress, noting who is able to hold form better than others and correcting those who need it.

"You keep dropping your right arm too soon," I correct one of the troops, a man named Jarek, stepping in and positioning him correctly with my own hands. "You are leaving yourself open to a return blow."

"Sorry, sir." He sighs as he holds position.

"Keep at it," I encourage. "You are improving every day."

"Thank you, sir," Jarek says, sounding more upbeat. "I will."

I smile as he slips back into formation with the others. Seeing people become more confident in their skills is one of the most rewarding parts of my job. I want to help every person serving under me to reach their full potential.

"Looking good, Captain." My husband, on the other hand, just enjoys watching the men work up a sweat.

"Don't you have better things to do besides being an old pervert?" I challenge as I approach the wall he is leaning against.

"You're one to talk, getting hands on with your men," he teases.

"Only doing my job," I reply innocently, leaning against the wall to join him.

Rurig hums to himself, eyes falling back on the troops. Even if my intentions were not entirely pure - which they are - this is not a subject that would upset my husband. It is not something that has happened recently, but in the past bringing a third person into our bed was not all that uncommon. Jarek just happens to be someone who has managed to catch both our eyes the past few weeks.

He is an attractive younger man, slightly shorter and much thinner than either of us. He is also easily ten years our junior, if not more. He is a hard worker and eager to learn, but there is an innocence about the way he carries himself. I have seen him getting along well with his fellow recruits, but he seems quieter and more content on his own.

Later that night, when the trainees are having their meal break, I spot Jarek at a table in the mess hall by himself. While most of the troops are loudly conversing with one another, he is using one hand to eat while the other flips the pages of a book. After grabbing some food for myself (and with a little prodding from Rurig), I approach him.

Orlun

"Is this seat taken?" I gesture to one of several empty chairs at his table.

"No sir. By all means." He quickly sits up and closes his book, and I feel a pang of guilt for disturbing him.

"I apologize. I did not mean to interrupt." I nod my head toward the book.

"Oh, that's nothing important." He shakes his head. "I've read it dozens of times."

"Is it a good book?" I've never been much of a reader myself, but Rurig is. "I assume it must be if it has you sitting here by yourself."

"It's an old favorite." Jarek smiles shyly. "Am I screwing up badly enough to require extra attention, sir?"

"No, nothing like that." I chuckle. *Not that you aren't worth my extra attention.* "Though I did notice you seem less eager to be here than some of the others."

"Ah. Well, the truth is, I've never really been much of a fighter," he admits, rubbing the back of his neck. "I mainly joined because it seemed like the right thing to do; I want to help protect my home and the people in it. But I also had a lot of...*encouragement* from my parents and older siblings."

"Ah, familial pressures." Though my parents are no longer with us, it is something I am all too familiar with. "Well your intentions are noble, and you are a fast learner. Do you have other family members in the militia?"

"My father *was* a member, and my two older siblings still are. It's not that I don't want to fight. I've just always been more interested in things like... Plants. Or building things. Or reading." He holds up his book as an example.

"There's nothing wrong with that." I offer a smile. I may be a warrior, but that is not something everyone is

7

built for. "You have met my husband. I would hardly call him a fighter."

"Is this old man bothering you, sweetheart?" The man's voice rings out from behind my back.

"Heh, no sir. Just eating dinner together." Jarek chuckles with a small blush.

"Uh-uh, he's sir." My husband lays a hand on my shoulder. "I'm Rurig."

"Well, the food is delicious as always, Rurig," Jarek says with a small bow of his head.

"Aww, you sweet talker. Let me know if you want seconds." Rurig winks. *He has always been the better flirt, which combined with his cooking skills makes him nearly unstoppable.* "So is this one boring you with his old war stories?"

"I wouldn't call them boring," Jarek defends with a grin. "I love hearing about the trouble the officers would get into when they were still new recruits."

"Oh, you want to hear about trouble?" Rurig responds with an even wider grin. "The first time we met, he suggested we—"

"*Attention!*" Captain Burningmaw calls out as he enters the mess hall, causing those in attendance to stand and face him. "Scouts have just located one of Warhunter's camps northeast of the city. Finish eating and suit up. We leave in half an hour!"

Everyone springs into action. Those who had finished their meals already quickly gather their used dishes while everyone else begins to quickly finish their food, the sounds of metal utensils scraping across the wooden plates filling the air. Across from me at our table, Jarek is doing neither, staring down at his plate in light shock.

Orlun

"I've... I've never actually been in a battle before." He suddenly looks very nervous. "What if... What if I mess up? What if I—?"

"Hey." I reach across the table, steadying one of his shaking wrists. "It will be alright. This is what we have been preparing you for. Just listen to your Commander, remember your training, and you will be fine."

"He knows what he's talking about, kid." Rurig walks around to place a hand on his shoulder. "You're gonna go out there, kick some ass, and be back here with your book in no time."

"Right." Jarek nods to himself. "This is what I've been training for. I can do this."

"Yes, you can." I squeeze his wrist once more. "And I am looking forward to hearing *your* first war story when you return."

"Looking forward to telling it to you, sir." He salutes before standing and exiting the mess hall, his appetite no doubt killed by nerves.

"He'll be fine, Papa Bear," Rurig reassures me, calling me by an old pet name. I can only nod and hope he is right.

After everyone leaves, the headquarters are significantly quieter. Without anyone to train, there isn't much for me to do. I busy myself with organizing the equipment, and with no remaining mouths to feed, Rurig is doing the same with the food stores. Even though neither of us is saying anything, we are both anxious to see Jarek and the others return unharmed.

Several hours later, just as the two of us are deciding that we need to get home for the night, we hear the guards at the front gate giving a cheer as the troops return. They seem to be in high spirits with minimal injuries and a number of Warhunter's men in tow. I scan the faces of everyone as they make their way inside, relaxing when I see Jarek. Everyone splinters off, some to handle the arrested rebels, and others to the showers or mess hall, but Jarek does neither, spotting me and Rurig in a corner of the training yard.

"How was it?" I ask as he approaches us.

"Incredible and terrifying all at the same time," he starts to explain, his voice bursting with barely restrained excitement. "The closer we got to the camp, the more nervous I got. It was so dark, but even with us trying to be stealthy, they saw us before we saw them."

"They attacked first?" Rurig asks.

"They got the jump on us," Jarek confirms with a nod. "I didn't even realize it until the guy in front of me went down. The rebel was right on top of him, and then it was like time froze. All my fear was gone because someone was in trouble and needed help."

"Moments like that can really define a person," I say with a smile. *I knew his training would kick in.*

"All I could think about was stopping the guy, so I pulled out my staff and leapt at him," Jarek continues, practically bouncing in place. "He was barely able to deflect my blows when I took him out with a strike to the back of the head. And then it was like my body was moving automatically—I could hear and see people fighting all around me, and I just started moving to help. It was like I had all this energy. I could feel the blood rushing through my veins. I wanted to... I wanted to..."

He suddenly reaches for my head, pulling me in for a deep kiss, then seconds later pulls away shocked.

"Oh spirits." His eyes are wide, looking between me and Rurig. "I am so sorry. I shouldn't have—"

Orlun

"Think we should take this back to your office?" Rurig asks me, amused as he takes in my surprised face.

"That depends." I manage to shake off the surprise. "Do you want to come back to my office with us, Jarek?"

"I... Yes." He quickly nods his head, looking between us both. "Yes, I would."

As Rurig takes him by the wrist, I lead us into the building that contains my office. No one else I share it with should be here this late, so it should serve our purposes nicely. We manage to avoid running into anyone else on the way, and I am happy to not have to deal with any awkward conversations as a result. Once we are inside, I lock the door behind us.

"Are you sure this is okay?" He looks at us both for confirmation.

"Kid, we've been married for over a decade. You're hardly the first guy we've snuck off with," Rurig assures him as he steps in closer. "Definitely one of the cutest, though." Taking Jarek by the chin, he leans in for a kiss of his own.

I watch as Jarek's eyes flutter closed as my husband deepens their kiss, the man's tongue probing into his mouth. Rurig was not incorrect about us bedding other men together, and my arousal only grows as I watch the two of them. When they finally split apart for air, I quickly pull Jarek over and slot our mouths together for my own turn.

As we kiss, Rurig moves to stand behind Jarek, sandwiching him between us. I can feel the young cub's nerves start to return as our hands roam over his body. Rurig's hands reach around his body, stroking over and then lightly pinching both of Jarek's nipples through his shirt, making him gasp into my mouth. His own hands

11

tentatively reach out for me, feeling the muscles of my chest and arms.

I break our kiss with a smile, turning Jarek around to face Rurig, who happily resumes his own kissing. I stroke my hands down Jarek's back, scratching it with the blunt of my nails before reaching for his ass. I squeeze him gently with both hands, snaking them around to his front and feeling his growing cock through his pants. *Not bad.* As I trail my thumb through the top of his waistband, his body goes still.

"Is this alright?" I ask Jarek with a kiss to his neck.

"Y-yeah." He nods a little fast.

He leans back against my chest as my fingers work to undo the buttons of his pants. Taking a step back, Rurig assists with untucking his shirt, his own fingers teasing the inside of the boy's underwear. Once I've finished with the last button, Rurig grips his pants and underwear, pulling them down together in one smooth motion.

Rurig makes a low whistle. "Lookin' good, kid." I look down over his shoulder to watch as my kneeling husband assesses Jarek's size.

"Not bad at all. We will have to see how we measure up." I grind my crotch against Jarek's ass for emphasis.

"Yes, sir," he responds breathlessly.

"I prefer Orlun when I've got my hand around your cock." I grab him lightly around the base and squeeze as I slip out from behind him.

Rurig and I push Jarek back, encouraging him to sit against a desk before I reach into my pants to fish out my own cock. As I take a seat next to him, I can feel Jarek's eyes lock onto me, fully hard and pointing straight out. I'm larger, both in length and girth, and at first glance, my size can be somewhat intimidating.

12

Orlun

"Go ahead and touch," Rurig encourages. "It won't bite."

"It's massive," Jarek comments absentmindedly as he strokes my thick length. "I-I'm not sure I could take something like that."

"If I can do it, so can you," Rurig tells him with a wink.

"Perhaps we will save that for another time." I doubt either of them are prepared for something like that at the moment anyway. "Right now, I am far more interested in seeing what my husband is able to do with what you've been waving in his face."

Jarek sucks in a gasp as Rurig wraps his lips around the man's prick, taking my words for encouragement. Humming happily, he reaches a hand over to grasp me, stroking slowly as he growls around the appendage in his mouth. I know from personal experience that my husband is an *excellent* cocksucker. Rurig takes Jarek all the way down to the hilt, forcing him to bite his lip as he holds back a moan.

Pulling off, Rurig shuffles on his knees to face me and gives a repeat demonstration. Knowing what I like, he takes his time, suckling on my head before swallowing down the rest of my shaft. I let out a low groan, my hand gently fisting the back of his hair on instinct as his throat muscles constrict around me.

"Fuck," Jarek whispers. "That is hot."

With a hungry grin, I pull Jarek against me on the desk, plundering his mouth with my tongue as Rurig works my cock. After a few more moments of bobbing on me, he switches back over to Jarek with a wet slurp. He swaps his mouth between us every few minutes, as hungry as I have ever seen him. The longer this goes on, the closer I feel myself getting, and the more ragged Jarek's breathing becomes.

"I think I'm...getting close," he tells me between kisses.

Hearing this, Rurig hums in excitement, his head bobbing even faster. I tease one hand down Jarek's chest, pinching a nipple as Rurig tries to push him over the edge. The closer he gets, the tenser his body grows until, with a whine, he cums. He shudders as he unloads into Rurig's mouth, who is no doubt still working his member.

"Knew you'd be tasty," he says with a smack of his lips.

"That was..." Jarek mumbles, his eyes still closed.

"We're not done yet," Rurig continues. "Why don't you get down here and help me take care of my husband?"

"I... Yeah, I can do that." Jarek nods, still in a daze, before pulling his pants up enough that he can kneel next to Rurig.

With both men on their knees in front of me, my cock gives an involuntary lurch, a fresh bead of pre-cum emerging on the head. A hand on his neck, Rurig pushes Jarek toward my cock while nestling himself right under my balls. Jarek looks up at me shyly with his lips around my shaft, or at least tries to, and I feel my hips jerk a little at the prospect of going deeper into the heat of his mouth.

I close my eyes and lean my head back as the two of them work in tandem, wet mouths sucking and nibbling at my skin. They switch places after a minute, Rurig swallowing me to the hilt without blinking an eye. I groan low as I grip Jarek by the hair and hold him tightly to my crotch, his tongue lathing over my testicles. Rurig is soon pistoning his throat up and down the length of my shaft, bringing me closer and closer to the edge.

Just as I am about to reach climax, I pull Rurig off and quickly begin to stroke my cock with my hand. Knowing what I am aiming for, my husband throws his arm over Jarek's shoulder, pulling him close and giving me a larger target. As the orgasm rolls through me, the first shot of cum sprays over the younger man's face, and the second across my husband's cheek. I shower them both equally with the remainder that follows, and Jarek takes me into his mouth when I am done, sucking the last drops from my head. For a moment, all three of us are in an exhausted daze, doing little more than catching our breath.

"You stay right there," Rurig orders as he shakily stands a few moments later. "This will only take me a minute."

He pulls out his own cock, stroking himself very quickly. Knowing how to help my husband along, I reach over and use one hand to roughly pinch at his right nipple. He tilts back his head when I bring my mouth to his neck, allowing me better access to kiss and bite at the sensitive flesh. Already in position, Jarek takes the initiative to suck on the man's heavy sack, my husband giving a jerk when the tongue makes contact with his skin. Not thirty seconds later, Rurig adds his load to mine on Jarek's face, muttering a curse to himself as he cums.

As my husband catches his breath again, I help Jarek to stand, pulling him in for another sloppy kiss and realizing too late that I now have both my and Rurig's cum on my face. I almost recoil when I feel the cool wetness hit my skin, but truthfully I could not care less.

"That was...amazing," Jarek vocalizes what I think we all are feeling as Rurig stretches his legs.

"Just wait until next time, kid." He nudges into his side and gives another wink before going in for a kiss of his own.

"There's going to be a next time?" Jarek asks the both of us hopefully.

"I certainly hope so," I answer with a grin. I really, really do.

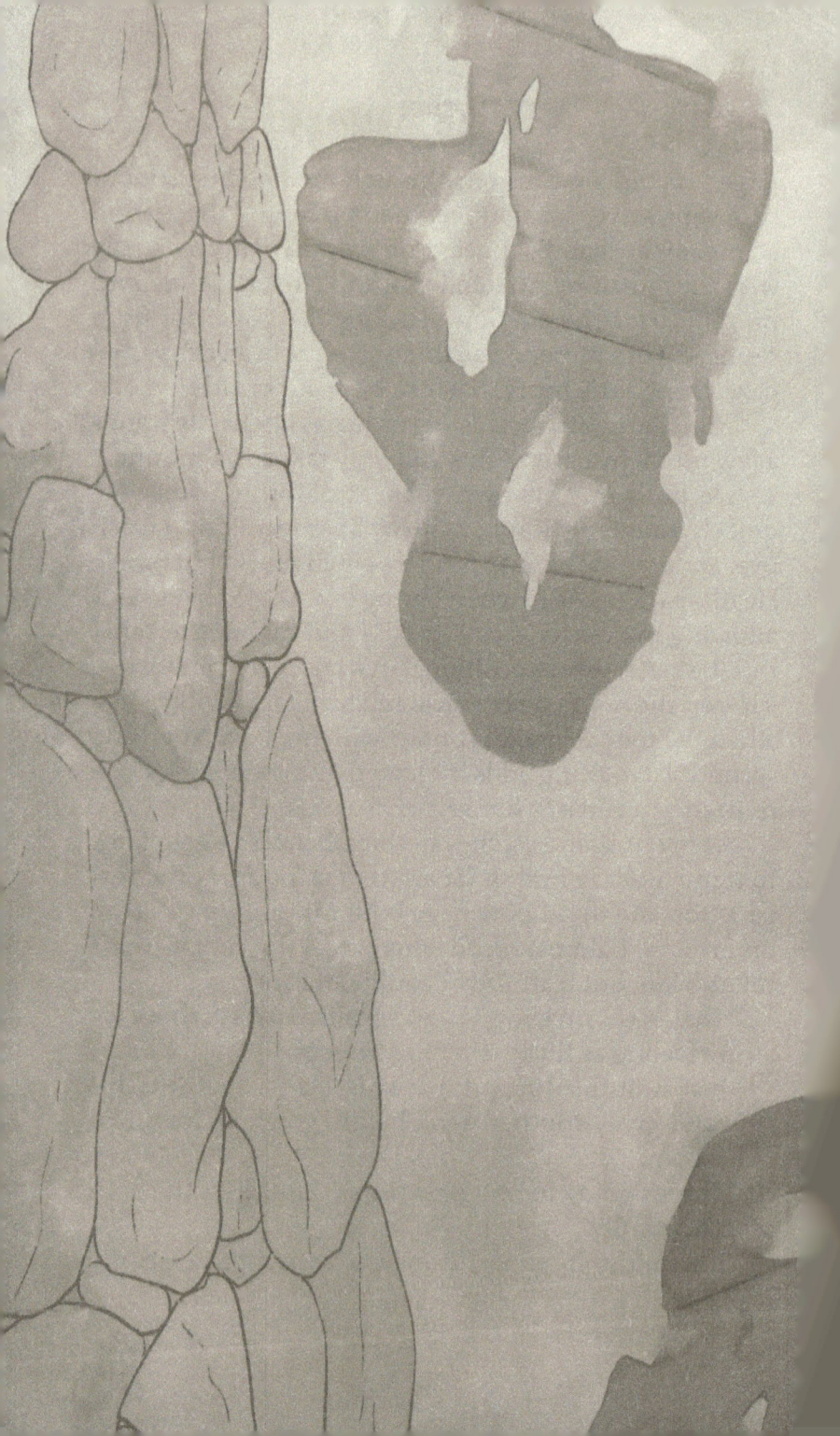

Chapter 2

Rurig

"**A**re you sure my hair looks alright?"

"I told you twice—you look fine," I tell Orlun again with a sigh. "Come on. We're going to be late."

It is dark as we rush through the city's streets, the sun having set hours ago. After finishing our respective shifts at militia headquarters, we left for our destination as fast as we could. We would not *need* to be rushing, had my dear husband not insisted on an extensive pre-shower grooming session, complete with trimming both of our facial hair.

He would never admit it, but he's nervous. I do not blame him because for some reason, I am too. It's silly because all we are doing is going to see Jarek at his home where we are most likely going to have sex—which we've already been doing for the past week. Sure, he is preparing a meal for us, but when you think about it, I have already done that for him dozens of times by now.

I actually offered to prepare the food myself, but Jarek insisted—another thing that is not helping this feel any less like a date. Which I suppose it might be? To be honest, it is hard to tell. We've been married for almost a decade, and it's been a while since either of us has done anything even resembling a date. What? Between the two of us, we have three kids and four jobs!

Meeting Jarek has been an unexpected and very pleasant surprise. Orlun and I had both taken notice of the quiet and thoughtful young man early on, but we never expected him to be attracted to two old hairy beasts like us. But he certainly has been; there has not been a single night since meeting him that we haven't spent some part of with him.

That is part of why I am so confident when I say we will be having sex tonight. One of the main reasons we are going to his home is because it is an actual house with a bed. As much fun as we have had, there are only so many times you can have sex in a cramped office before it loses its thrill. There was also one time in the showers, but after almost being walked in on by one of Orlun's rangers, we decided it would be best not to risk it.

Heh, it was very much worth the risk at the time, though.

"Are you *sure* I look alright?" Orlun asks me nervously as we approach the address Jarek gave us.

"Calm down, Papa," I tell him while scratching my fingers up and down his back. "We're only here for some food and some fun."

"I know." He sighs, still nervous.

We're in the southeastern part of the city, not that far from a tavern we used to visit. The house is small, like most of the houses around here are. It is a single story with two windows greeting us on either side of the door. It actually reminds me a lot of the first home I shared with Orlun. Stepping forward, I knock on the door twice and stand next to my husband, pretending not to be just as anxious as he is while we wait for Jarek.

Rurig

"Great! You made it," he answers cheerily before opening the door wider. "Please, come in."

"Sorry we took so long," Orlun apologizes as we enter, and I hold back from making a joke about it being his fault.

"Thank you for having us over." I give Jarek a small kiss as I pass him.

The home is as small on the inside as it is on the out- side. Nothing extravagant but just what I would expect for someone his age. We are standing next to a couch in the simple-looking living room. There's a small kitchen attached to the back of the room, and we can smell Jarek is already cooking.

"I know it's not much," Jarek says somewhat bashfully after closing the door behind us.

"You have a perfectly lovely home," Orlun insists.

"I'm not sure I would go that far," Jarek responds with a chuckle. "I share it with one of my brothers. We're just living together to save money."

"It can be nice to have family around." I look around the room, trying to see if I can tell which objects belong to which brother. "And tonight he is...?"

"On duty," Jarek answers with a grin. "Whereas I am not."

"Wonderful." I give him an equally devilish grin.

"Speaking of wonderful, whatever it is you are cooking smells amazing." Orlun sniffs the air. Food is one of the easier ways to my husband's heart. I am 90% sure it was my cooking that got him to propose.

"Just a venison roast. Nothing fancy," Jarek downplays. "It still has a while to go, so I thought maybe we could do some things to work up an appetite while we wait."

"I like the way you think." I saunter over to the young chef, pulling him toward me by the hip and capturing his mouth in a kiss.

Jarek hums happily against my lips, opening automatically when my tongue swipes over them, seeking entrance. As I deepen our kiss, I feel Orlun's presence as he moves to stand at our side, his hand touching the small of my back as he watches us. When Jarek and I finally separate, Orlun quickly moves in for his own kiss. Then he repeats the same on me, his hand moving down to squeeze my ass with a growl.

The three of us stand there in the living room, swapping kisses and getting increasingly handsy with each other. Three-way kissing is something I have witnessed once between two elves and a human, but sadly tusks don't really allow for it.

"How about we take this into the bedroom?" Jarek asks breathlessly after Orlun has finished kissing him senseless.

"Hear that, Orlun? We've been good enough to earn a bed this time," I tease with a cheeky grin.

Jarek rolls his eyes at me as he turns and leads us from the room down a short hallway. We pass a door on our right that opens to the bathroom as Jarek enters the room at the end of the hall. There's a room on our left that I can't help but peek into as we follow him, seeing a fairly plain-looking bedroom, at least when compared to Jarek's.

The first thing I notice about his bedroom is the bookcases, all six of them. Each one is filled to the brim with books of different sizes and colors, some sticking out more than others. There is a set of drawers against one wall and a desk against another with more books stacked in one of its corners, along with writing utensils in a small clay cup. Then there is the bed, which is large enough for two to sleep, but should also be large enough for three to fuck. *Heh.*

"Well, this is it," Jarek announces as we both take in the room. "Like I said, nothing special."

"It is lovely," Orlun insists, stroking a hand down the young man's back.

"Yep, lovely. Now take off your pants." I smirk as I get right to the point.

"You first," he responds with a smirk of his own.

"Happy to." I am already undoing my belt even as my husband groans at my crassness.

"C'mon, you too." Jarek presses Orlun, his hands moving toward his pants to start the process himself.

"If you insist," my husband says with a fake huff, kissing Jarek again as he allows the man to unbutton his fly.

Once we are both pantsless, we take a look at each other, unable to hold back a laugh at how ridiculous we look still wearing our shirts. We quickly tear those off as Jarek strips off his own clothes to join us in our nudity. While he works, Orlun takes the opportunity to kiss me again, scratching down my back with the blunt of his nails before squeezing my ass with both hands, just the way I like.

"I will never get tired of seeing that," Jarek says as we break apart. "Sit on the bed, please."

He pushes both of us back, hands grabbing at both of our growing erections as we sit on the edge. He kneels down, stroking us both to full hardness as he looks back and forth between our cocks. Orlun and I share a knowing look before wrapping one arm each around the other's backs, squeezing together.

Just so he doesn't get any ideas about the pecking order here, I tug Jarek's head toward my cock before he has a chance to suck down Orlun first. What? I was the first person with his pants off. It's not like he fights me even a little bit, happily wrapping his lips around my rock-hard prick.

I sigh happily as I feel the warm mouth enveloping me, closing my eyes as I lean my head to the right against my husband's shoulder. I stroke my hand loosely through Jarek's hair as he begins to slowly bob up and down on my length. I feel one of his hands wrap around my heavy sack and manage to fight off the urge to hump into his mouth—for now.

I open my eyes when I feel him pull off, watching him shuffle over to Orlun, who up until now he has been stroking with his free hand. Jarek starts to stroke me now as Orlun takes his turn occupying his mouth with a growl. Looking down, I watch as my foreskin is pulled back on each downstroke. My arm still around his back, I turn to face my husband who is already turning himself, our mouths meeting in the middle for a hungry kiss.

As we probe each other's mouths, Jarek moves back and forth between our cocks, keeping his hands wrapped around whichever is left swinging in the open air. I no longer fight the urge to hump into his mouth, hearing the occasional gag when I push a little too deep. I relish the feeling of his throat squeezing my prick, and Jarek is no less eager for more.

Though it may be hard to believe, I *do* eventually have enough of this. Not Jarek—I just mean I'm ready to move onto other things. After another minute or so of sucking my cock, I push him off gently, standing and pulling him to stand. After kissing him quickly and tasting Orlun and myself on his tongue, I swap our positions and push him onto the bed, his cock standing straight up as he sits down. *My turn.*

As my husband can attest, I *love* sucking dick. I also happen to be damn good at it. Kneeling between Jarek's legs, I place both hands on his thighs, leaning forward and capturing his erection with my mouth. I easily swallow him down to the hilt, my nose pressing against the dark forest of curly hair at its base. Jarek groans in surprise, grasping blindly at my head while I squeeze his thighs with both hands.

I pull back and swirl my tongue around his head, capturing the taste of his pre-cum before taking him into my throat once more. I love feeling the weight of him in my mouth and the scent of his musk I inhale when I'm at his base. While I give Jarek one of the best blowjobs of his life, to my left, I see my husband's legs moving as he turns onto his side toward us. The muffled noises I hear moments later tells me Orlun is kissing Jarek again, helping me to attack our boy with pleasure at both ends.

Once I've had enough of his cock (for now), I decide it's time to move on to greener pastures—specifically the green pasture of Jarek's ass. While they hang over the edge of the bed, I grab both of his legs behind the knees and lift. There's a muffled noise of confusion, but Orlun realizes what I am trying to do and assists me by grabbing one of his legs and holding it back. Still holding his other leg, I watch his tight, furry hole twitch in the air before finally diving in.

Jarek's whole body shudders when he feels my tongue swiping over his hole. I start slowly, making small circles around his rim with the tip of my tongue. As I add more and more pressure, I can feel the ring of muscle opening up, beckoning me farther inside until I'm spearing him with my tongue as the flat of my tusks press against his skin.

Jarek moans as I fuck him with my tongue, doing his best to push against me while lying on his back. My cock hangs heavy between my legs, and I reach my free hand down to give myself a squeeze as I hungrily devour his hole, the wet, smacking sound of my lips on his skin echoing through the room. I close my eyes as I continue to eat him, losing myself in the heat of the moment. I only realize Orlun has stepped off the bed when I feel him tapping my shoulder.

"I think I would like a turn at that, dear." He looks down at me in amusement.

"He is all yours," I answer with a grin, wiping my mouth with the back of my hand and standing, letting Jarek's feet fall to the floor.

Orlun captures my mouth in a kiss, no doubt tasting Jarek on my tongue. Then he kneels down in my former position, lifting Jarek's legs again before eating his hole with just as much enthusiasm as I had. I watch transfixed, stroking my cock as Jarek writhes on the bed under my husband's ministrations. Then I start to get ideas for what comes next.

"Jarek, where do you keep the—"

"Oil is in the top drawer." He points at the dresser. "I already used the charm." *Someone is eager.*

I turn and retrieve the oil, noting the location of Jarek's cleansing charm in the drawer before I close it. I pop the cork on the bottle and pour some out into my hand and stroking it over my dick as I return to the show my husband is putting on. I don't get to see him doing this very often, given that I am usually the one on the receiving end of it.

When Orlun has finally had his fill and stands, I hand him the bottle with a smirk, knowing he'd like to go first. While he slicks himself up, I take the opportunity to do the same to Jarek. With his legs still in the air, I rub my slick fingers over his hole before slowly pushing one inside. He groans at the stretch, his toes curling slightly as I pump it in and out a few times before adding a second.

Satisfied that he is prepared enough (probably even more than he has been during any of our quick trysts at headquarters), I step aside for my husband to move into position. Sitting on the bed, I run my dry hand over Jarek's chest while I watch Orlun take aim at his hole. As he pushes in on his target, Jarek gives a gasp of surprise when Orlun finally pops in, his body going tense for a moment.

Pushing his legs back with both hands, Orlun sinks the rest of the way inside Jarek. He groans happily, pausing to give the younger man time to adjust to the intrusion. Jarek looks up at Orlun in slight awe, my husband pressing a gentle kiss to the inside of his ankle. After letting the two of them make eyes at each other for a bit, I lean in, turning Jarek's face towards me and once again kissing him senseless.

Orlun begins to slowly pump his hips, causing Jarek to bounce each time they meet. As he picks up the pace, the sound of their skin slapping together fills the room. While I kiss him, I see one of Jarek's hands moving down to grab his cock, which is a deep, dark green as it lies hard and leaking against his stomach. He might like getting his ass filled almost as much as I do.

Soon enough, it's my turn, Orlun sliding his hands up my thigh to get my attention. Breaking away from his face, I move between Jarek's legs, my cock still slick with oil. I look at my husband's handiwork, the wet, open hole clenching around the open air, eager to be stretched again. Pressing the head of my cock against his opening, I rock my hips forward and do just that.

Spirits, that is nice. All warm and wet with just the right amount of tightness. I love getting inside of a hole after Orlun's gotten them good and opened up. I am not quite as large as he is, so I watch with a grin as my cock easily slides in all the way to the base. I lean my weight against the backs of his thighs, pressing as deep as I can go and pulling a groan from Jarek's lips.

While I start to drive my cock in and out of the tight ring of muscle, Orlun takes up my previous position on the bed and keeps Jarek's upper half occupied. We continue like that for a few minutes until we switch again, and then again. By the time we swap a third time, Jarek is a needy mess, his hand no longer touching himself to keep from cumming before he is ready.

Ready for a change myself, I stand from the bed and return to the dresser. I retrieve Jarek's cleansing charm, pressing it to my belly and allowing the magic to do its work. Then, while Orlun and Jarek watch me, I grab the bottle of oil, this time reaching behind myself to apply it liberally to my hole. Then without a word I climb onto the bed next to Jarek, presenting my ass to the air.

"Trying to tell me something?" Orlun asks with a smirk, still lazily pumping into Jarek.

"It just looked like so much fun." I give my ass a shake.

Orlun chuckles as he pulls out of Jarek, the smaller man taking the opportunity to stretch his legs. Stepping

Rurig

behind me, my husband teases my ass with his prick, running it up and down my slick crack. Each time he passes over my hole, I push back, trying to capture him with my ass. Finally, he takes pity on me and pushes inside.

If the way to my husband's heart is through his stomach, then mine is through my ass, and seeing as Orlun prefers to be on the opposite side of things, we are very well matched. I moan happily to myself as he fills me, letting my chest fall to the mattress once I feel the familiar scratch of his hair against my rear. He knows exactly what I like and how to do it.

Orlun immediately starts to fuck me, giving me no time to adjust like he did with Jarek. That is alright because I do not need time to adjust—I am more than used to taking my husband's cock. Hell, I could probably take him with nothing but spit, but as it is, he's nice and slick, driving in and out of my hole and rubbing right over that one spot inside that drives me crazy. I reach underneath myself to grab my cock, stroking myself slowly.

Orlun keeps fucking me until suddenly he's not, and when I look back to complain, I see Jarek stepping up. That shuts me up, turning back around and presenting my ass once more. After taking me in both hands and squeezing, he spreads me wide, cock aimed straight for my entrance. He's smaller than Orlun, and his technique is a little faster, but that doesn't mean it feels any less good.

I lose track of time as the two of them take turns on me, not even bothering to look and see who is currently inside of me—I can tell from the way they feel. This is much longer than any session we've been able to have before, and I intend to milk it for everything it's worth. Just like the two of them are doing to my prostate.

"Hold on," Orlun says, pausing before slipping out of me. "Rurig, move farther up the bed. I want to try something."

I'm always game for trying something new, so I do as requested, crawling up the bed toward the headboard. Next, Orlun has Jarek climb up behind me, where he sinks right back into my hole without even needing to be told. *Good boy.* I feel the weight on the bed shift again, but I don't realize what Orlun is doing until I hear Jarek gasp, right before he is pushed even deeper into my ass.

"*Spirits*," I hear Jarek gasp above me, his cock never once flagging. "So good..."

"Aww, are we finally too much for ya, boy?" I taunt Jarek by squeezing his cock with my hole.

"Just... Don't want to cum yet..." I can hear the struggle in his voice as the pleasure continues to build.

"Then you had better hold on," Orlun warns from his spot in the back, right before snapping his hips, fucking Jarek into me.

As Orlun starts to fuck faster and faster, I realize quickly that Jarek is not going to last very long. I reach for my cock, stroking myself with a firm hand and working myself toward the same edge he is riding. Each time Orlun pumps forward, Jarek bottoms out inside of me, the added stretch making me moan. He's not able to move much, only the little bit of space he has between Orlun and me, but it's more than enough for me.

"Gonna...cum..." he announces, pushing Orlun to fuck him even faster as he spills over.

I feel the heat of his cum spreading inside of me as he starts to unload. Each time Orlun snaps his hips, I feel another spurt of warmth. As Jarek shudders and twitches above me, I find my own orgasm, moaning as I shoot onto the mattress, my hand still moving rapidly over my cock. Orlun is right behind us, growling as he breeds Jarek deeply with enough force to shake the bed.

As we all come down from our orgasms, Jarek bends over to lay on my back, not quite collapsing. The air in the room is thick and hot, and I know each of us is covered in sweat. Certainly smells nice. The mattress shifts when Orlun finally pulls out of Jarek, collapsing onto his side next to me. With a little effort (and an angle shift that causes him to slip out of me), I manage to lay flat on my stomach with Jarek lying on my back. For a moment, time seems to stand still, the three of us just laying together, listening to nothing but the sounds of our breaths and our heartbeats.

Then Orlun's stomach growls.

"Apologies," he says with a blush. "I seem to have worked up an appetite."

"Oh shit, I almost forgot about dinner!" Jarek suddenly pushes off of my back and rushes from the room.

"That was wonderful," Orlun tells me as we walk home, either late at night or early in the morning, depending on how you want to look at it.

"Are you talking about the food or the sex?" Seeing as I left with both my stomach and my hole full, I would agree with either.

"Both," he concurs. "Though that roast was the perfect meal after everything else." He rubs his stomach for emphasis.

"It was pretty good," I concede. "Not as good as anything I could make, but maybe I can pass along a few pointers to the boy some time."

"Oh? Are you saying you want to spend more time with him?" he teases me with a twinkle in his eye.

"Maybe I—"

My words are interrupted by the sounds of an explosion ripping through the air, the ground giving a small rumble.

"What was that?" I ask, looking around in the sky for the signs of a fire.

"I do not know," Orlun answers, sounding worried. "It came from the north in the forest. There shouldn't have been any militia operations out there tonight."

"What do we do?" *I'm just a cook!*

"I need to gather whoever is on duty and find out what happened." Orlun has already put on his Captain hat. "Go home and check on the children. I will be back as soon as I can."

"Be careful," I tell him, pulling him close. "I love you."

"I love you, too." He kisses me softly, doing his best to disguise his worry. As he heads off, I say a short prayer to the Three for his safety and turn toward home. My only thoughts now are on my children.

I'm up for hours waiting for Orlun to come home, checking on the children nervously every time my mind starts to wander to dark places. It's after five o'clock in the morning when I hear the front door open, Orlun walking in still wearing his ranger uniform. He looks tired and not just physically. Something is wrong, but I wait for him to undress before attempting to broach the topic.

"What happened?" I ask when he finally takes a seat in the living room, next to me on the couch.

"It was...terrible," he starts, shaking his head. "The explosion. It was Ahyoka."

"What?" I don't understand. "The elf woman who helped with investigating that cave that was uncovered last summer? Little Nylan's mother?" Khazak and Ayla had come home talking excitedly about the new half-elf, half-human student at school, and we quickly made the connection.

"The same." He nods somewhat numbly. "She is dead."

My eyes go wide. "How? What happened?"

"We are still trying to figure that out." He runs a hand through his hair. "From what we have gathered, about a dozen people came to her home late in the night and... took her. We only know that because of her son, who was there when it happened. She hid him. In a *chest*. He was still in there when we came to investigate the home."

"What?" My blood turns cold, my thoughts immediately turning to our own children. "Is he alright?" I immediately wince at my stupid question.

"He's traumatized," Orlun answers wearily. "Barely speaking. I felt bad even prying that small amount of information out of him. The current assumption is that the kidnappers have ties to Warhunter. We suspect they may have been trying to ransom her, perhaps to her family in Pákannon, but we cannot be sure. It will take some time to piece together exactly who they were."

"Were you able to get a description out of Nylan?" That seems like too much for such a young boy after such trauma.

"No, we have them. The kidnappers." His voice goes icy. "In pieces. The explosion *was* Ahyoka. She cast a spell that blew herself and the rest of them up."

"*What?!*" I can't help my volume and immediately clamp my hands over my mouth, worried about waking the kids. "Why? Why would she do that?"

"We don't know." Orlun shakes his head. "Her husband has said that though she had some raw talent, she was by no means a trained spellcaster. Maybe the spell was stronger than she anticipated. Or perhaps they surprised her and she cast it by accident. Or maybe she just knew she wouldn't get away. I do not know."

"...How is her husband? Atsadi." My husband knew both of them better than I did, having worked with them briefly when they were studying the cave ruins.

"He completely blames himself for the two of them being home alone while he worked an overnight guard shift with the militia." That poor man and his son. "I tried to reassure him that it wasn't his fault, but all I could think about was... What if those people had come to our house?"

"*Spirits.*" I run my hands through my hair. "I can't even... We weren't even *home.* They would have just come in and taken... What were we thinking, Orlun?!"

"I don't know." He shakes his head. "They're *children* for spirit's sake, and we expected them to what—look after themselves? There is practically a war going on outside!"

"And now we have to explain to them why their friend's mother is dead." I sink lower in my seat and my guilt. "What have we been doing? We are terrible fathers."

"I wish I could disagree with you." Orlun sounds as defeated as I feel.

"I'm quitting. Today," I decide without a second thought. "The militia and maybe even the restaurant." *Buying a one-way ticket for Port Stay-at-Home Dad.* "I don't care if anyone complains."

"Good." Orlun nods, not that I doubted his support. "I am going to reduce my hours as well. If they cannot understand after this, I'm not going to care either. You and I have to do better."

"We will." I take his hand and squeeze. *We will.*

Chapter 3

Jarek

"Why do you keep staring at the front gate?"

"Huh? Uh, no reason." *Shit, am I that obvious?*

I try not to look embarrassed as I look away from the gate, not liking that I was caught by one of my fellow recruits. *I think her name is Hiruk?* I'm gonna have to work on that. The staring thing, not the name. I thought Rurig was supposed to be here a few hours ago, but he wasn't in the mess hall when I checked. I don't know why I'm feeling so anxious. I saw them both just last night. I must just...want to make sure they had a good time.

I mean, I had a great time. With dinner *and* the before-dinner activities. But it also felt different. Like something between us changed. *Ugh, what am I talking about? It was dinner and sex. Not even in that order. It was nothing. Just*—I'm distracted from my thoughts by movement at the entrance. *Thank the Three, they're here, and I can stop talking to myself.*

They both seem worried when they come in through the gate. I don't approach them to find out why because again, I'm trying not to look obvious. I don't want the other recruits to think I'm getting special treatment or something. They're looking around, and when Rurig's eyes finally fall on me, he smiles—for a second, before quickly frowning, and then trying to look neutral. He nudges Orlun, who looks at me and does the same. *What did I do?*

They don't keep me waiting, both making their way toward me. Knowing we won't have a ton of privacy here, I move away from where I'm leaning against one of the outer walls of the barracks, farther away from my fellow recruits. The way they both look at each other when they reach me, as if they aren't sure who should start, makes my heart sink.

"Jarek..." Orlun starts, saying my name with concern.

"Is everything alright?" *Better start building that wall back up.* "Sir?"

"Everything is fine," Rurig quickly jumps in, his soft voice trying to reassure me.

"I apologize." Orlun grimaces. "It has been a very long day. And night."

"*Shit*, right, the kidnapping and...explosion in the forest." I forgot that Orlun, as Ranger Captain, would have been the one to deal with all that. *He must have been up all night.* "Sorry, it sounded awful."

"It was, and there is still much left to do with the investigation." Orlun sighs unhappily.

"*Rurig!*" All three of us turn to our right to see Pulmin, another cook, exiting the mess hall. "Where have you been?"

"I better go take care of this," Rurig tells us with a grimace. "Sorry, kid."

"It's okay," I tell him as he walks away from us and into the mess hell.

Jarek

"Actually, I think he may be apologizing for more than just that," Orlun sounds reluctant to continue. "You may be seeing less of us around here in the near future."

"What?" My voice goes high-pitched at the new information. "I will? Why? I thought everything was okay." *Spirits, calm down.*

"Yes, everything *is* okay with us," he starts to reassure me. "It is just that, after last night, we—"

A loud explosion suddenly shakes the ground beneath us, and Orlun and I both nearly lose our balance. *What the hell was that? Oh spirits...* It came from the mess hall. The windows have all been blown out, smoke starting to pour from the holes.

"*RURIG!*" Orlun shouts, already running toward the building with me and several others right behind him.

Spirits, please let him be okay.

The scene inside of the mess hall is horrific with bodies thrown against the walls by the force of the blast. As the room fills with smoke, we try to locate the injured and pull them outside. Orlun manages to find Rurig under a flipped over table, unconscious and with his foot a mangled, bloody mess.

By the time everyone is out of the building and the fire extinguished, we have a little more information, but no real answers. From what the still-conscious could tell us, an unknown person entered the mess hall and pulled an object from his robe, casting a spell that then caused the explosion. As he was at the center of the blast, he obviously did not survive, or else we would have already started interrogating him.

Naturally, it is assumed that this was an attack by Warhunter's group. Given the "explosion," people are already suspecting a connection to last night's attack in the woods—though Orlun seemed skeptical. Rurig was taken with the rest of the injured to the healer's while the rest of the militia got to work relocating any important supplies to one of the two ranger stations, where they will be based until the militia headquarters has been repaired. I expected to be assisting them, but Orlun told me he needed my help with something special, and then led me to his and Rurig's house.

"You want me to *what*?" My eyes go wide, making sure I just heard his request correctly.

"Look after our children," he tells me again as we stand in front of Rurig and his home.

"I didn't even know you *had* kids." I look between Orlun and the house—that apparently has children in it.

"You did not?" He looks at me, surprised.

"No! You have literally never mentioned them. Neither of you." *Although I guess I can remember hearing some talk about the Ranger Captain and children in the past...*

"I did not realize," he responds sheepishly. "I am sorry. We have three. Two sons and a daughter."

"Oh." I'm not really sure what to say. "I don't know the first thing about kids. What happened to their normal babysitter?"

"They...do not have one." *What? Then who's been watching them while their dads have been at work?* He looks at me pleadingly. "Please. I would not ask if it were not important. I need to go be with Rurig at the healer's and do not want to leave them alone with everything that has happened in the last twenty-four hours."

"I...Alright, I'll watch them." I can't say no. I don't want these kids to be alone, and I don't want Rurig to wake up at the healer's alone either.

Jarek

"Thank you. Thank you so much." The look of relief on his face helps too. "I will introduce you before I go."

"Probably a good idea," I mumble to myself. *What am I getting into?*

"Khazak, Ayla, Yogik," Orlun calls out after opening the front door and leading us inside.

"Orda?" A young voice calls out from the hallway.

A small green head pokes out from the side of the doorway. A little boy it looks like. After seeing his father, he rushes into the room and is quickly followed by two other children, a girl and an even younger boy who toddles as he walks. Orlun kneels down as they approach, embracing and squeezing them against his chest in a tight hug.

"We heard a loud boom," the little girl tells him. *Shit, they must have heard the explosion.*

"Where is Ruda?" the boy asks, realizing Rurig is not with Orlun.

"Who is this?" the little girl asks next, noticing that I am in the room.

"This is Jarek," Orlun tells her, releasing them so they can look at me. "He is a good friend of mine and Ruda's. Jarek, this is Khazak, Ayla, and the little one hiding behind Ayla is Yogik."

"Hello." As I wave awkwardly over Orlun's shoulder, Yogik cowers behind Ayla's back.

"Where is Ruda?" Khazak repeats, eyeing me suspiciously.

Orlun pauses, looking at his children thoughtfully before speaking. "Ruda is with the healer. He was hurt."

"Ruda was hurt?!" Ayla cries out. Yogik immediately starting to bawl behind her.

"Yes, but he is going to be okay," he tries to reassure them. "I am going to go be with him now while Jarek looks after you."

"I thought I was in charge," Khazak looks down, sounding disappointed. *He was in charge?!*

"You have done a great job, little one," Orlun tries to comfort his son. "But it will be safer with Jarek. It is just until Ruda and I get back."

Khazak doesn't say anything, just nods, still looking at the floor.

"Is Wuda okay?" Yogik speaks his first words through sniffles, hugging his father again.

"Yes, I promise." *I'm no parent, but I don't think that's the kind of promise you make.* "We will both be home soon."

"Okay." Yogik sniffles and allows his father to stand.

"Thank you again." Orlun turns to me with a hug. "I cannot tell you how grateful I am."

"Just...hurry back soon, okay?" I hug him back.

"I will," he tells him with a chuckle before kneeling down to hug his children again. "Your father and I love you all very much."

"Love you too, Orda," Khazak says first. "And tell Ruda I love him, too."

"I love him too!" Yogik repeats next. "Tell him, Orda. Please."

"Tell him I love him the most," Ayla finishes, all three of them holding on to their father as long as they can.

"Behave and listen to Jarek," Orlun tells them after standing. "Ruda and I will be home soon."

With a final sad smile, he exits the home, closing the door behind him. Alone with the kids, I walk into what appears to be the den with couches and an unlit fireplace in one corner.

Jarek

"Was Ruda hurt bad?" The question from Ayla catches me completely off guard.

"He..." *Spirits, that didn't take long. I should lie to them, right?* "He's going to be just fine."

And the truth is, I do think he will be. In the immediate aftermath of the explosion, the biggest concern with him and several of the others was blood loss from their wounds. I have very, very low-level nature magic, and along with some of the others, I was able to use that to stop the worst of it. The healers should have an even easier time. But when I think about the state his mangled foot was in... *Not the time to think about that.*

"How did he get hurt?" Khazak's question throws me off even more than his sister's. "Was it the loud boom?" *DO NOT ANSWER THAT!*

I look at a clock on the wall, groaning mentally when I see that it is still far too early to feed and put them to bed. Probably. "What do you usually do together before dinner?" I ask, sidestepping the question entirely.

"Play games, tell stories," Ayla starts counting on her fingers. "Take turns changing Yogik's diaper."

"Don't wear diaper anymore," Yogik tells her, his tiny eyebrows scrunching together in anger. "I like colors."

"He means coloring. Like art," Khazak informs me, still looking very unhappy. "We have chalk, but we're not allowed to play with the paints without Orda or Ruda."

"Oh, sometimes we practice our archery in the backyard!" Ayla tells me proudly.

"We're not supposed to do that without Orda or Ruda either," Khazak corrects her.

"You weren't supposed to tell him!" She stomps her foot on the ground.

"How about we play a game?" *Because the Three them-selves could not convince me to give these tiny monsters equally tiny weapons.* At least this will hopefully distract all of us from thinking about Rurig.

"Okay. I'll pick!" Ayla rushes over to a low shelf on the opposite end of the room.

"Not *gornop!*" Khazak chases after her. "You always pick that one."

"You just don't like it because I always win," Ayla taunts her brother.

"Only because you always cheat!" Khazak challenges, shouting in her face.

"I do not!" Ayla yells back in his.

"You hide extra tokens in your pocket and add them to your pile when you think no one is looking." *Damn, this kid is observant.* "I counted last time."

"Maybe not gornop?" I call over, trying to defuse the situation.

They seem to accept my request, with Ayla wearing a frown—which grows when Khazak sticks his tongue out at her. *What did I agree to?* While his older siblings fight, Yogik has been shyly watching me from behind a large throw pillow he's holding in his lap. It's honestly pretty adorable.

"We can play *tuk-tuk!*" Ayla announces, holding a small wooden box in the air.

"Fine, we can play tuk-tuk," Khazak acquiesces with a grumble.

"Do you know how to play?" Ayla asks as she places the box on the low table between the couches before opening it.

"I do, but I'm not very good," I lie, my gaze wandering over to Yogik, who immediately hides behind his pillow.

Jarek

"Do you wanna help me? Be on my team?" At his age, he probably isn't very good at board games, if he understands them at all.

He peeks out from the side of the pillow, biting his lip before nodding. With a smile, I pat the seat on the couch next to me, watching as he slowly slides off of the other couch and climbs up next to me. While Ayla sets up the game board, Khazak takes a seat on the couch where Yogik was, still frowning and glowering at his lap. I swear, he looks like a tiny, grumpy version of Orlun.

Tuk-tuk is a very basic children's game. After selecting a small wooden token, each player starts at a different location on the board, an equal number of spaces apart. The tokens are usually carved into the shape of an animal and painted a solid color; Ayla chooses a red cardinal, Khazak a gray wolf, and I let Yogik pick out a coiled green snake for the two of us.

At the start of their turn, the player rolls the dice and moves their piece forward, hoping not to land on any of the trap spaces along the way. Things like mud bogs, rope traps, and pitfalls will leave a piece stuck for one or more turns while everyone else continues moving. When one player's piece overtakes another, that player is out, with the game's ultimate goal being to overtake all of the pieces on the board and be the last one standing.

I let Yogik roll the dice for our team of two, which more often than not he does with more force than is needed, sending them flying to the floor. I help him move our little green snake around the board, counting the spaces out loud and then asking him about the space we landed on. I can't exactly say I'm having fun, but it's pretty cute.

The kids at least seem to be enjoying themselves, for the most part. Yogik squeals and claps excitedly each time we land on a space that isn't a trap, and I can see Ayla's competitiveness coming out as the game progresses. Khazak, however, has continued to scowl from his seat on the couch since we started. It almost seems like he's angry to be playing this, and I even catch him glaring at me once or twice.

"You never told us what happened to Ruda." I freeze at his sudden question, half bent over the board.

"I, uh..." Shit, that didn't last long. "I'm not sure I should tell you."

"Is it really bad?" Ayla asks, her voice filled with concern.

"Is Ruda okay?" Yogik looks at me, his eyes already starting to water.

"Nono, your Ruda is gonna be just fine. I promise," I try to calm him down quickly. "The healer will look at his foot and—"

"What happened to his foot?" *DAMMIT!* Khazak's question cuts me off before I can say more, but it's too late—Yogik starts bawling.

"Look what you did!" Ayla chastises her brother, walking around to Yogik.

"I didn't do anything!" Khazak argues. "Yogik never cried when *I* was in charge." He stomps his way out of the den, slamming the door on what I'm guessing is his bedroom.

"It's okay, Yogik," Ayla helps me to calm her younger brother. "Orda and Ruda will be home soon and everything will be fine. Right?" She looks to me for confirmation.

"Right." I nod, really hoping that I'm not lying. "...How long have you all been staying home alone at night for?"

"It feels like forever..." She worries her lip as she thinks. "It started right after Orda came home and said Mr. Warhunter did something bad."

Jarek

"Spirits..." I mutter to myself. They've been alone the *entire rebellion*? What were Orlun and Rurig thinking!

After Ayla and I manage to stop Yogik's crying, there is little to be done about salvaging our game, especially with Khazak pouting and refusing to come out of his room. So, I decide that it's time to make dinner, leaving Ayla and Yogik to entertain themselves for a little bit. After what Ayla told me, I think they can handle a few minutes alone in the den.

I search through the kitchen's two ice boxes for something suitable. There's what looks like precooked meals Rurig probably set aside for the children, cubed meat that looks like it's been seared in a pan, but I still have to find something for myself, and end up settling on a simple sandwich made with some sliced pork.

I spend far too long looking for matches to light the oven with before remembering I can just use magic. I can get a little forgetful in high-stress situations, and I think this definitely qualifies. It's not every day you're only meters away from an explosion that kills and maims several of your friends and comrades and are then asked to look after the three children of your sorta-lovers, one of whom was hurt in the aforementioned explosion.

"What are you doing here?" I ask myself out loud. I can't help but bark a laugh in response. If I stop and start to think about it, it feels like I'm losing my mind. Not that I'm going anywhere; I'm not cruel. They're children and they clearly need someone to look after them.

I can't believe I didn't remember they were parents. I mean, they obviously don't talk about their children much, but Orlun's the fucking Captain of the Rangers. It's public knowledge. I wonder if that was intentional. Did they think it would scare me off? I mean, it might have—I'm not exactly loving the situation they've left me in.

I have no idea what kind of parents they are. Only that they seem to be perfectly fine leaving their three young children home alone—during a war, even if no one is calling it that yet. Fuck, didn't I hear they found a kid last night, too? Seriously, what were they thinking?

"Who the hell leaves an *eight-year-old* to look after another eight-year-old!" I say out loud in frustration, running my hand through my hair.

I hear a sudden noise on my right and turn my head, just barely catching the sight of Khazak's head leaning in the doorway. He has a hurt look on his face, but before I can say anything, he turns and runs away. I hear the slam of a door as he holes up in his bedroom once more. *Great job, Jarek.*

I manage to finish heating the kids' dinner without any other issues, but eating together is still plenty awkward. Yogik doesn't seem to notice as he happily and messily chews and swallows, but the other two are quiet. Khazak is still wearing his scowl as he silently pushes the food around his plate.

"May I be excused?" he asks after barely eating anything.

"Sure," I answer, not knowing what else to do.

Not long after, Ayla and Yogik both finish, and I handle the clean-up while they go back to entertaining themselves because I'm pretty sure that's what babysitters are supposed to do. Afterward I look at the clock, and it seems late enough for bedtime, at least for the three-year-old.

"Will you read me a story?" he asks, right back to the timid little boy I saw hiding behind his sister.

Jarek

"Sure." I've never tucked someone in before, but it turns out I don't mind it so much. Especially not when he asks for a bedtime story. I love reading.

He picks out a book from the tiny bookshelf in his room, *The Hunter and the Fox*, a classic children's tale. As I read aloud about the cunning fox sending the hunter on a wild chase through the forest, Yogik begins to slowly nod off, sound asleep before I'm even halfway through the story. Sliding the book back onto the shelf, I exit the room, closing the door quietly behind me.

Ayla and Khazak follow not long after that, Ayla insisting she does not need to be tucked in, and Khazak not saying anything at all. Which leaves me in the den for the rest of the night, alone with my thoughts. I spend the first half of the night doing very little sitting as I pace around the room, going between worry about Rurig's condition to annoyance with him and Orlun for putting me in this position. That goes on for a few hours until finally at some point, I pass out on one of the couches.

The next morning, there's still no word from Orlun or anyone else for that matter. I'm not really sure what to do. It's technically a school day, but I doubt Orlun would want me sending them if they're even open after everything that's happened the last two days. I certainly don't think I'd send my kids out after the militia base was attacked.

That leaves me to figure out breakfast, and then lunch, all while trying to keep the kids entertained or at least from biting mine and each other's heads off. It doesn't take long for the worried questions about their fathers' whereabouts to start up again either, and I feel as though I might go insane with stress when there is finally a single knock at the front door.

"*Orda!*" All three children cry in unison when the man enters the den. *Thank the Three.*

"Hello little ones." He kneels down to embrace his children. "I missed you. How are you?"

"We're okay, Orda," Ayla answers for her siblings. "Where is Ruda? Is he okay?"

"He is fine. Just still resting with the healer," he tells them as he straightens his posture. "We are hoping he will be well enough to bring home in the morning."

"I miss Wuda," Yogik tells his father, pouting.

"I know, Yogik." He pulls his son in reassuringly. "He misses you too."

"Are you staying, Orda?" Khazak asks his father as he stands up.

"Yes, at least for a little while until I need to go see your father again," he answers with a smile. "Now go and play. I need to talk to Jarek for a bit."

The kids nod reluctantly as Orlun pulls me into the kitchen so we can speak with some privacy.

"Thank you again for doing this." He hugs me, and I find it a little difficult to hug him back right now.

"Is Rurig really going to be okay?" I'm really hoping he wasn't just bullshitting his kids in there.

"Yes, though…" He grimaces before continuing. "They had to amputate his foot."

"What?" *Oh no.*

"There is a healer in Pákannon that is supposedly skilled enough to regrow lost limbs, and the militia offered to pay for his services, but Rurig insisted that the money and the healer would be better spent taking care of the rest of the injured or any future victims." He huffs an annoyed laugh. "Damn prideful fool. They are fitting him with a prosthetic tomorrow."

Jarek

"Fuck." It feels like the wind has been taken out of my sails. "Is he okay? Mentally, I mean?"

"Yes, at least he claims." Orlun nods sadly. "He says that he is fine, but I know he is more upset than he is letting on."

"That sounds like him." I can't help but smile at that. At least for a second. "I'm glad he's alright but..."

"What?" Orlun watches me, concerned.

"What exactly has been going on around here?" *Time to get that wind going again.* "You have *three* kids? And you've been leaving them alone while the city turns into a warzone?"

"Excuse me?" He's taken aback by my change in tone. "I understand that you are upset over only just learning about them, but that is not—"

"No, I'm not upset about that," I quickly correct him. "I mean, it is weird that neither of you ever brought them up even once, but I'm talking about the fact that you left three kids whose combined ages are far less than mine home alone to take care of themselves. What were either of you thinking?"

"I'm sorry. I did not realize you were a father." He sneers at me. "Who exactly are you to tell *either* of us how to raise our children?"

"The guy you left them with at a moment's notice!" I fire back. "A complete stranger to them, I might add!"

"You do not know the first thing about my children!" he shouts in response.

"That's my point!" *Aaaaaand now we're both yelling.*

"My children are just fine!" He looks and sounds pissed off now. "They are more than capable of handling themselves."

"Yeah, they seem really fine." I roll my eyes. "Your youngest son is completely terrified while the oldest is stuck acting like an angry brat!"

Of course, right then is when we both hear a noise, and we turn and see that Khazak is once more eavesdropping on whatever is going on in the kitchen. Not that I blame him since we are basically yelling. But still, I feel even shittier when he runs off a second time after hearing me talk about him like that. *That kid* definitely *hates me now*.

"You have *no right* to tell me how to parent my children." Orlun pokes me in the chest to regain my attention.

"You know what? You're right. I don't." I bat his hand away, turning and walking toward the door.

"Jarek, wait—" he calls out.

"Have a great fucking life, Orlun." As I slam the door behind me, I lie to myself, thinking that I'm more than happy to no longer be part of it.

Chapter 4

Jarek

Knock on the door, Jarek. Just lift your hand and hit it against the wood. That's all you have to do. It's not a big deal. You've done it a million times! So just do it. Before people start to wonder what the hell you're standing out here for.

It's the middle of the afternoon, and I'm standing in front of Orlun and Rurig's home, staring at their door. It's been over a week since the last time I was here. Since Orlun and I fought. Since Rurig was hurt... Maybe this was a bad idea. They have bigger things to worry about than me.

The rebellion only officially ended days ago. I wasn't part of the climactic final battle or anything. I wasn't even on duty the night when Warhunter's location was discovered, and they made the final push—inside the city walls. The fighting is over, but there's still plenty of cleanup going on. Since the danger has passed, I'm no longer officially a part of the militia, but I have been volunteering where I can.

I actually already tried looking for Orlun at the militia headquarters—the temporary one set up in the main ranger station. Rangers on duty told me he hadn't been in all week—he was home caring for Rurig. So, ignoring the stab of guilt in my chest, I thanked them and headed down here. I've been alternating between standing and pacing in front of their door for what feels like an eternity but realistically has probably been around fifteen minutes.

Yeah, this was a terrible idea. There's no way they'd want to see me right now. I should just go. Just as I'm making the decision to leave, the doorknob starts to turn. *Oh, shit.*

"Jarek?" Orlun is surprised to see me, which hopefully means he doesn't know how long I've been out here. "Is everything alright?"

"Orlun, hi." I wince at the casual tone of my voice. "I—Yes, everything's okay."

"I was just going to check the mail." He points toward his mailbox near the road. "It is good to see you."

"It's good to see you, too," I tell him honestly. "I was just in the area, and I wanted to..." I start to trail off, suddenly nervous.

"I'm sorry—"

"I'm sorry—" We both blurt out at the same time, stopping just as quickly. Orlun motions for me to continue first.

"I wanted to apologize for what I said the other day," I start to say. "You were right. I had no right to tell you how to raise your—"

"No, *you* were right." He doesn't let me finish. "About leaving the children alone, about the way I dumped them on you, everything."

"It's... It's okay." I say what it feels like you're supposed to say, even if it sounds like nonsense.

"No, it really isn't." He sighs and shuts the front door behind him before leaning back against it. "Yogik starts to bawl if he's so much as in a different room as me or Rurig, Ayla has been waking up almost every night with nightmares, and Khazak will barely speak to any of us. I am a failure as a father."

"You're not a failure." That's easier to say because it's true. "You just made some mistakes."

"You know, we were already planning to cut back our hours so the children would no longer be alone." He looks up at me with a sad smile. "That is what we wanted to talk to you about, right before..."

The bombing in the mess hall. "Well, that's good. You guys were already trying to do better."

"Fat lot of good it did us." He shakes his head with a cynical chuckle.

"How is Rurig?" I decide to move on to hopefully happier news.

"He is doing well." His shoulders relax, and he gives me a real smile. "Or as well as he can be. He has healed just fine but is still getting used to the prosthetic."

"Have you been able to get him to rethink finding a healer to regrow his leg?" Such capable healers are rare, and it would probably be expensive, but it's still possible.

"We've discussed it, but Rurig insists that the money can be better spent elsewhere." He smiles at his husband's stubborn nature. "I think he is also put off by the excruciating pain that would no doubt come with reopening the wound."

That's true. Technically his leg has already been healed, and the only way to regrow something that is already healed—like an improperly set bone or missing a limb—is to reopen the wound. I assume that is exactly as painful as it sounds.

"Well I'm glad he's doing alright." I could have found out about days ago if I had just come to see him.

"Would you like to come in?" Orlun asks hopefully. "He's missed you. We both have."

"...Yeah, I'd like that." I'm suddenly full of nerves again. "I missed both of you, too."

There are thankfully no more awkward words, just another smile as Orlun reaches back to the door, holding it open as we both walk inside. I've only been here once, and it ended pretty badly, but I feel a pulse of warmth knowing that I'm back in their home. I let Orlun lead me from the entrance into the den, where Rurig is seated on one end of the couch.

The man is wearing a robe looking a little dour, and I can't exactly blame him. Unable to help myself, my eyes immediately go down to where the bottom of his robe opens, where his missing leg would be, taking in the wooden prosthetic in its place. It's a thick and sturdy looking rod made of dark brown wood, starting at the scarred skin under his knee, going straight down, and then turning at a 90-degree angle where his foot would be and curving upward slightly.

"Jarek?" He instantly brightens when he notices me behind Orlun. "It's so good to see you." He starts to try and stand, grabbing a cane with one hand and pushing off the couch with the other.

"Let me help you." Orlun rushes over when he sees him start to struggle.

"Leave me alone." Rurig tries to shoo off his husband's fussing. "I'm never going to get used to the damn thing if you don't let me."

"You are not supposed to push yourself," Orlun grumbles but leaves him be.

Jarek

"I'm just standing up!" Rurig huffs as he straightens himself before turning to me and hobbling forward, grinning. "It's so good to see you."

"It's really good to see you too." I embrace him in a hug, instantly feeling the way he has to shift his weight because of his leg. "I'm so sorry about—"

"Hey, did you set the bomb?" I look at him in shock, shaking my head no. "Then you don't have anything to apologize for. This was because of Warhunter and his friends."

"Then I'm sorry for not coming to see you sooner." I let him go slowly, making sure he has his balance.

"Orlun told me about what happened." He grimaces but tries to give me his signature grin anyway. "I was starting to think that our terrible parenting scared you off for good."

"I'm sorry." My turn to grimace. "It was a lot, and there was so much going on..."

"You have nothing to apologize for," he tells me again, Orlun coming up behind him and shaking his head in agreement.

"I could have come by sooner," I argue. "Just to see how you were."

"Well as you can see, I am doing just great." He tries to strike a little pose, holding up his cane—and loses his balance.

"I've got you," I tell him after catching him, Orlun and I both rushing forward when he stumbles.

"Thanks," Rurig grumbles from my hold.

"It's good to see you, too," I tell him with a chuckle.

"We really *did* miss you," he admits as I help him stand.

"And I missed the both of you," I repeat what I said to Orlun. "How have you been?"

"Oh you know, as fine as can be," Rurig gives me the non-answer as Orlun helps him back to the couch.

"I already told him about everything outside," Orlun tells him as he takes his own seat.

"You're supposed to tell me that *before* I lie," Rurig grumbles. "*Okay*, not fine," he admits. "It's like learning to walk all over again. Not to mention how much of a bitch it is to get pants on."

"Well, it's barely been a week," I encourage. "The first time you learned to walk had to take almost like a year, right?"

"*Spirits*, I hope it doesn't take that long." He leans back, looking up at the ceiling. "I couldn't go back to work now if I tried. Good thing I was already planning on taking time off, right?"

"Yogik is certainly happy about it," Orlun says with a sigh. "Attached to our hips. We only just got him to take a nap ten minutes before you arrived. I think this is the longest we've been alone in days."

"It's a small price to pay considering how much we haven't been around lately," Rurig adds guiltily.

"So... Is it just the three, or do you have any more secret children?" I tease, sitting on his other side.

"Kid..." He looks reluctant to continue. "We didn't mean to hide them from you. We just didn't think you'd want to hear about any of that."

"What he is *trying* to say is that... You are young." Orlun leans forward to look at me. "Part of us assumed that you would not be interested in romantically pursuing two men with a family. Especially now after learning everything else about our parenting."

"Hey, I'm not *that* young," I start, wanting to prove my intent to them. "I admit I wasn't exactly thinking long-term the first time we...got together. I don't like the way I found out about it, and I'm not saying I think leaving your kids alone like that is okay, but I've had a lot of time to think about things."

"Anything else you don't like, kid?" Rurig asks with a smile and a huff.

"Maybe don't call me 'kid,' seeing as you have *actual* kids." I nudge him with my elbow.

"I can do that," he agrees, "and you won't hear either of us arguing about being complete screw-ups as fathers."

"I don't think you're complete screw ups." The hyperbole feels like a defense mechanism.

"That makes one of us," Orlun says in response.

"No, really. You messed up, but it's not unfixable." *I know a thing or two about family troubles thanks to my own.* "I'm not trying to promise you anything, or get ahead of myself, but... If you'll let me, maybe I can try and help you figure some of it out."

"Are you sure that's what you want?" *That might be the most vulnerable I've heard Rurig ever sound.*

Instead of answering with words, I lean forward and kiss him. Even with everything that's happened, I still want them, both of them, messy family and all. I only hope they feel the same.

"You know... Yogik is probably gonna sleep for at least another hour." *I'm gonna take that hungry look as a good sign.*

"Does that mean you'd like to show me where the bedroom is?" I mean, if they're both up for it, so am I.

"Follow us," Orlun answers for his husband, helping him stand.

The two lead the way toward their bedroom with Rurig in front and Orlun right behind him. I can tell he's paranoid that Rurig might fall again, but he doesn't want to say as much. When we reach the door at the end of the hall, Rurig pushes it open with his arm, and I'm happy with what I see: a nice big bed, at least twice the size of mine.

The rest of the room is as you'd expect with a small table on either side of the bed, open chests filled with clothing, and a door to the bathroom off to the side. Rurig sits on the edge of the bed, laying his cane down flat on the floor and patting the spot beside him. Without any more delays, I take my seat, leaning over for the kiss I know is coming.

He quickly locks our lips together, so fast that I can hear Orlun chuckling above us when our tusks bump into each other. He steps closer, his legs brushing my knee as Rurig slides his tongue into my mouth. Not to be outdone, Orlun bends over once we break apart, taking his turn with each of us.

Already in an opportune position, Orlun's hands move to unbutton his pants and pull out his cock. Rurig reaches for it first, wrapping his fingers around the thick green shaft and squeezing lightly. Then, after giving me another grin, he leans forward and swallows it down. Seeing as there's still plenty of room, I join him, bending over and mouthing at Orlun's heavy sack.

I run my tongue over the skin of Orlun's balls, nuzzling against the furry bush at the base of his cock. *I missed the way he smells, too.* A hand moves to the back of my head, and I bet Rurig has one on the back of his as well. Orlun groans when Rurig takes him all the way down, and I can't help the silly giggle that escapes when our tusks once more bump together. A short while later, Rurig pulls off and grabs his husband's cock, pointing it at me.

Jarek

Not needing to be told twice (or even once, technically), I happily wrap my lips around Orlun's prick. Before you ask, yes, I also missed the way he tastes. I savor the stretch of my lips and the weight on my tongue as I bob up and down on his shaft while Rurig has taken my previous spot lapping at his husband's testicles. After another minute or two, we trade off again, and then again.

"Alright, I get to suck that dick every day," Rurig says after pulling off for a final time.

"Is that a promise?" Orlun asks, wet cock still dangling in front of our faces.

Rurig rolls his eyes, turning to me. "What I *mean* is that it's your turn." He slaps me on the thigh. "Get those clothes off and move up on the bed."

I am happy to comply, pulling off my shirt and tossing it to the side. I shuck my pants off and slide backwards up the bed as Rurig and Orlun both join me in undressing. Once he's naked, Rurig crawls his way up the mattress, stalking me like a hungry predator. At least until his prosthetic gets caught on the sheet at the edge of the bed, and he looks back, growling in frustration. He attempts to shake himself free but only manages to tangle himself further before he loses his balance and rolls onto his back, taking the sheet with him and trapping his legs in the fabric.

"I hate this stupid fucking leg!" Rurig yells at the ceiling in a way that tells me this is about more than just the sheet. He crosses his arms over his chest. "They should have just left me with a stump."

"Come on. You don't mean that." I kneel up and lean over, looking at his face upside down.

"He is right." Orlun works to untangle his husband's new foot. "It has not even been two weeks yet. You will get used to it in time."

"Easy for the two of you to say. You're not the one stuck looking like a pirate." He frowns grumpily.

"I'll have you know I happen to *love* pirates." I boop him on the nose. "Alright, change of plans—*you* move up the bed."

I roll to the side and let Rurig take my place at the head of the bed, which he does with some more grumbling. While Orlun watches these developments with interest from the foot of the bed, I take Rurig's previous spot, crawling between his spread legs. I place a kiss against the scarred knee on my way to his crotch, stroking over his thighs with both hands as I settle on my stomach.

I nuzzle against his crotch, kissing and licking my way up his shaft until I reach the head and engulf it. Rurig lets out a little moan as I start to suck, and I can feel the weight on the bed shift when Orlun joins us, cuddling up to his husband's side on my right. I hear the wet smacking of lips while I bob up and down on Rurig's cock and can feel Rurig's body relax underneath me as he is kissed and sucked.

I hum happily to myself as I make one of my two men feel good, enjoying the taste of his pre-cum on my tongue. I like that thought—my men. I've had a lot of time to think about it, and this is exactly where I want to be. I don't just mean between Rurig's legs, either—though that's pretty nice too. I'm not sure how long we go, but eventually my jaw starts to hurt, and I need to pull off and give it a rest.

"I think Jarek had the right idea," Orlun tells his husband. "I want you on your hands and knees next."

Jarek

"Oh, you're gonna be pushy too?" Rurig challenges, but he is already turning over as I move to the side.

"I could be less pushy if you were not so stubborn." He gives Rurig a playful smack on the butt.

After making sure he's in a comfortable position, Orlun moves behind his husband, grabbing the thick green rump with both hands. From my spot next to them, I watch as he kneads the flesh before parting it and lowering his mouth to his target. Rurig moans and shudders when the tongue touches his hole, and I reach down to give my plump dick a squeeze as Orlun starts to noisily eat out his husband.

"The oil and charm are in the bedside table," Orlun tells me after briefly pulling his mouth away from Rurig's ass.

I roll off the bed and retrieve the objects requested, liking where things are headed. After presenting them to Orlun, he wraps up his rim job and takes them, reaching under to press the charm to Rurig's belly before dribbling some oil down the crack of his ass. As Orlun massages it into Rurig's hole, I start to stroke myself slowly, enjoying the show.

"You just gonna sit there, or are you gonna get up here and feed me some of that?" Rurig looks over at me, and then down at my cock, suggestively.

I quickly and happily move up the bed, sliding between the headboard and Rurig's upper body. I spread my legs, letting Rurig close the gap between his mouth and my cock. He moans around me while Orlun continues to finger him open, the vibrations making my cock twitch.

He moans again a second later when Orlun starts pushing his slicked-up cock into his hole, holding his breath as he feels each centimeter sink inside, sinking down onto his chest. His eyes are closed, holding my cock in his mouth as he adjusts while Orlun's face is filled with pleasure as he savors the feeling of being buried in a warm, tight ass. Then the *real* fucking starts.

Orlun's thrusts start steady, his hands holding tight to Rurig's hips. Meanwhile, Rurig bobs up and down on my dick, swallowing me to the root and massaging the base of my cock with his tongue. As Orlun's thrusts get stronger, Rurig starts moving with them in time and letting that guide his mouth up and down my shaft.

I run my fingers through his hair, humping up to meet him halfway and feed my dick into his mouth. As I do, he slides one of his hands under me, giving my butt a squeeze before his fingers dive into my crack. I twitch in surprise when I feel my hole being teased but quickly push down against them. Rurig pulls them away, quickly spitting on them before bringing them back, this time gently seeking entry. I bite my lip as I'm breached with a fingertip, happily humping upward to feed Rurig more cock in exchange.

I lose track of time after that, the three of us doing whatever we can to stuff holes and play with pricks. I'm almost sweating by the time Rurig has his full finger inside of me, rapidly humping against his face, which is a saliva-soaked mess. He has been moaning almost continuously as Orlun gives him multiple anal orgasms with his thick hammer of a cock. He's even having another one now, his hands squeezing my thighs as the tremors roll through him.

I'm not expecting it, but I'm the first of us to cum as Rurig works his finger against my prostate. He seems to be expecting it more than I am as he has no problem swallowing down the load I shoot, still giving short, shuddering thrusts into his mouth. Orlun must have been waiting for me, or seeing me finish is what triggers himself, as he cums inside Rurig's ass with a low growl, hands still holding tightly to his hips.

Rurig, after having his ass literally wrecked, is more concerned with slumping down onto his belly and catching his breath, easily the sweatiest of us all. Orlun joins him, falling onto his side next to us and throwing an arm over his husband while squeezing my hand with the other. I slump back against the headboard, exhausted and content. After releasing all of those pent-up emotions (okay, and the orgasms), I think all I want to do is lie here and relax.

"*Ruda?*" A small voice calls out from somewhere else in the house—Yogik. He sounds scared.

"I better go get him before he gets upset." Rurig extracts himself from the bed with a groan, being careful of his foot and slipping on his robe. "I'm right here, cub," he calls down the hall as he exits.

"Are you sure you want to be a part of all this?" Orlun asks me with a laugh, though I can tell he's half-serious.

"Yeah, I do." I stand, offering him a hand.

After cleaning up—ourselves and the bedroom—we get dressed and find Rurig in the den playing a card game with Yogik on the couch. I'm not planning on doing anything else today, so I join them, and not long after that, it's time to start dinner. While Rurig instructs me and Orlun on how to prepare the pheasants in the kitchen, I can't help but think about how much I really don't mind all of this, being here with them and their family. Maybe being a part of that family.

"So, what were you planning on doing now that you are finished with the militia?" Orlun asks, sitting at a small table in the kitchen with Yogik on his lap.

"Remember how I mentioned that I like to do things with my hands?" I look at them both for confirmation, ignoring the eyebrow wiggle Rurig gives me. "Well, I was actually looking into taking an apprenticeship at Urgnot Nursery & Carpentry."

"Building homes and furniture? A respectable profession." Before Orlun can say anything else, we can hear a door being closed. "Ayla and Khazak must be home."

With Orlun carrying Yogik, I follow the two fathers to greet their two other children in the foyer. Unfortunately, both children already seem to be upset for some reason—Khazak even looks roughed up. Ayla at least smiles when she sees me, but Khazak looks shocked that I'm here and immediately turns and runs from the room, followed by a familiar sounding door slam.

"Ayla, what's wrong with your brother?" Rurig asks, looking in the direction he ran.

The girl looks down and kicks her feet, reluctant to answer.

"Ayla." Orlun kneels down, setting Yogik on his feet. "What happened at school today?"

"Murok Breezehollow was making fun of Ruda's foot." I can tell that even repeating that is making her upset again. "Khazak got into a fight with him... I almost did too."

"That little shit..." Rurig mutters.

"*Rurig,*" Orlun chastises. "Thank you for telling us, Wolfheart," he calls her by an adorable nickname I had not previously heard. "Why don't you get cleaned up and go play some before dinner?"

Jarek

"Okay, Orda," she tells him with a hug, followed by another hug for Rurig, Yogik, and even me—and yeah, maybe that makes me feel a little happy inside.

"We probably need to speak with their teachers," Orlun comments after picking Yogik back up. "Possibly the other child's parents as well."

"Oh, I got a few things I'd like to say to them," Rurig grumbles before calming down. "So, do you want to try to talk to Khazak, or should I?"

"He has barely spoken to either of us all week," Orlun answers with a sigh.

Spirits, I hope what I'm about to suggest does not turn out to be a terrible idea. "Do you think that maybe I could try and talk to him?"

"Do you think that would work?" Orlun asks, both fathers looking surprised.

"Maybe?" I offer, unsure. "If he's not willing to speak to either of you, maybe he will be with an outside person." *Even if he doesn't really like me, it's worth a shot.*

"If you are certain," Orlun says after silently conferring with Rurig. "Let us know if you need us."

"Will do." I hug them both and ruffle Yogik's hair.

I head for Khazak's bedroom, grabbing my bag on the way. I hesitate outside his door when I hear the quiet sobbing coming from inside. *Poor guy is really upset.* Steeling myself, I knock softly against the wood.

"Come in," he says after sniffling. He's lying in his bed and looks surprised when it's me who enters instead of his fathers. "What do *you* want?"

"I heard you had a rough day at school," I tell him, taking a seat in the too-small chair at his desk.

"School was *fine*," he lies, hugging his knees. "I don't need *your* help."

"I know you don't, buddy." *I think I'm going to have to try a different tactic with him.* "You must be a really strong and tough guy for your dads to leave you alone like they did." I move the chair closer to the bed.

"I thought I was doing a good job..." He sniffles, and something tells me there's more to that sentence than even he realizes.

"I think you did a great job," I try to reassure him. "So did your dads. They just wanted to be extra sure that you and your sister and brother were safe."

"But then Ruda got hurt." Another sniffle.

"Which wasn't your fault, Khazak." *Shit, is he blaming himself for* that?

This might be more than I can help with, but I might know someone who can. I need to remember to put Orlun and Rurig in touch with High Priest Azkosot. I'm not a religious person, but he helped me and my family through some of our own issues, when my parents were fighting all the time. I wouldn't have even half as good a relationship with my family if not for him.

I pause and look around Khazak's room, not having been inside it before. It looks pretty normal for a kid's bedroom: bed, desk, small hunting bows lined up on one wall. But there's also a bookcase that's almost filled to the brim. I stand, browsing through some of the titles, surprised to see some I would expect for someone a few years older.

"Do you like to read?" I ask, running my fingers across a row.

"Uh-huh." He nods, wiping his face with his arm.

"I like reading too," I tell him. "What's your favorite book?"

Jarek

"The Rangers of Red Mountain." I smile as I remember reading the action-and-adventure filled story when I was his age.

"I like that one too." I take a seat back in the chair. "It used to be my favorite. I read it *so* many times."

"What's your favorite book now?" he asks, and I say a silent *thank you* to the Three that if I couldn't help with the deeper issue, I could at least distract him a little.

"Oh, it's great! It's got adventure, and treasure hunting, and pirates." *I am so glad I grabbed my bag before coming in here.* "It's called *Treasure Island.* Do you want to hear some of it?"

He sniffles and nods as he slides over, silently clearing a space for me on the bed. I happily take it, cracking the spine on one of my oldest and most treasured possessions. I'm always happy to go on another adventure with Long John Silver. I bet Khazak will be too.

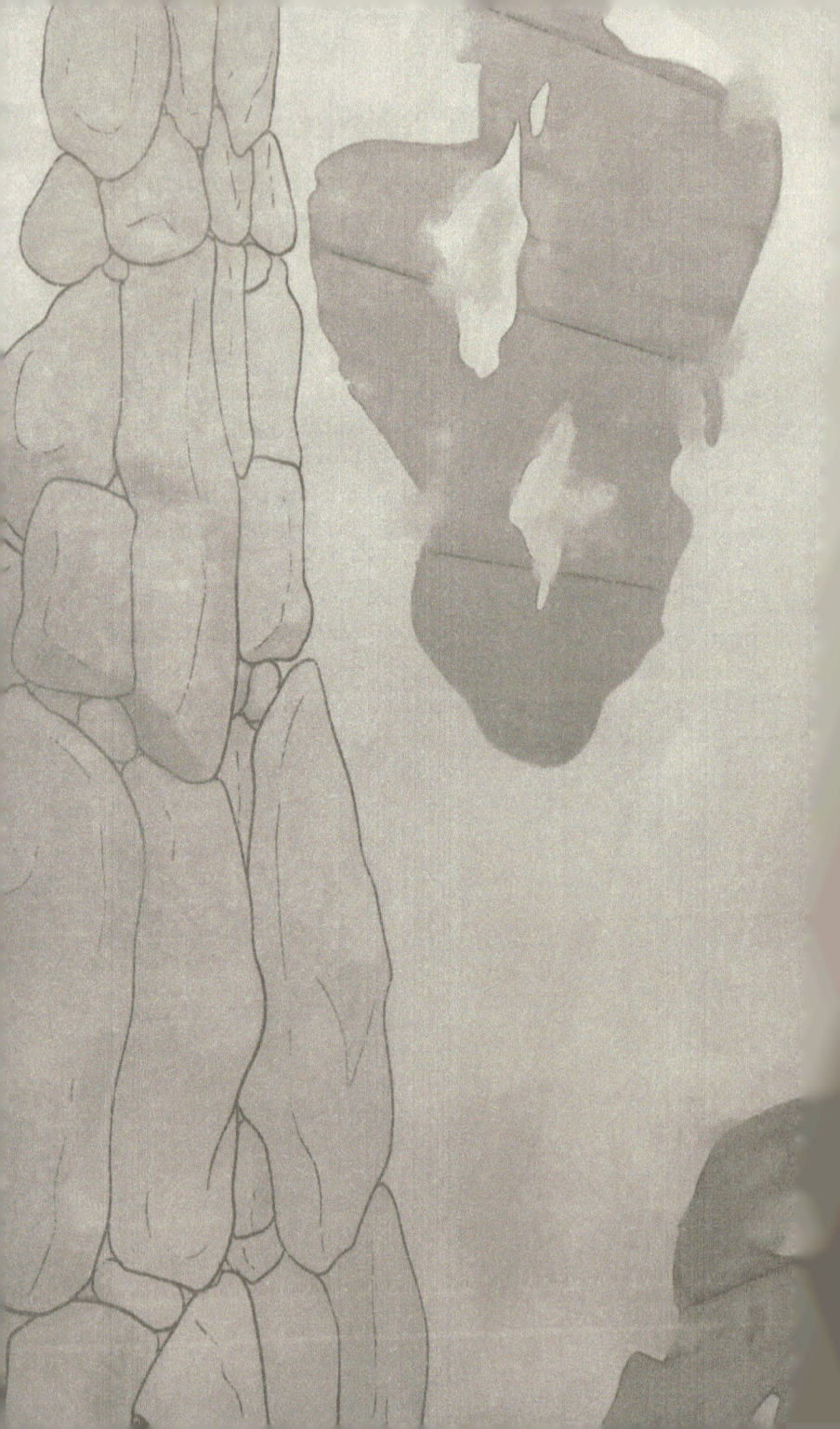

Before the Storm
Book Club Questions

1. Orlun and Rurig have been together for a long time and are comfortable in bringing Jarek into their relationship. Would you ever bring someone else into your own relationship or join an already established one?

2. How did you feel after learning that Orlun and Rurig were leaving their children home alone? How would you have handled things if you were in their shoes?

3. Jarek has an argument with Orlun that almost results in him no longer seeing the other men. Would you have said or done anything differently to avoid the fight?

4. Toward the end of the story, Rurig has a hard time dealing with his newly disabled status. How do you think you would handle losing a limb?

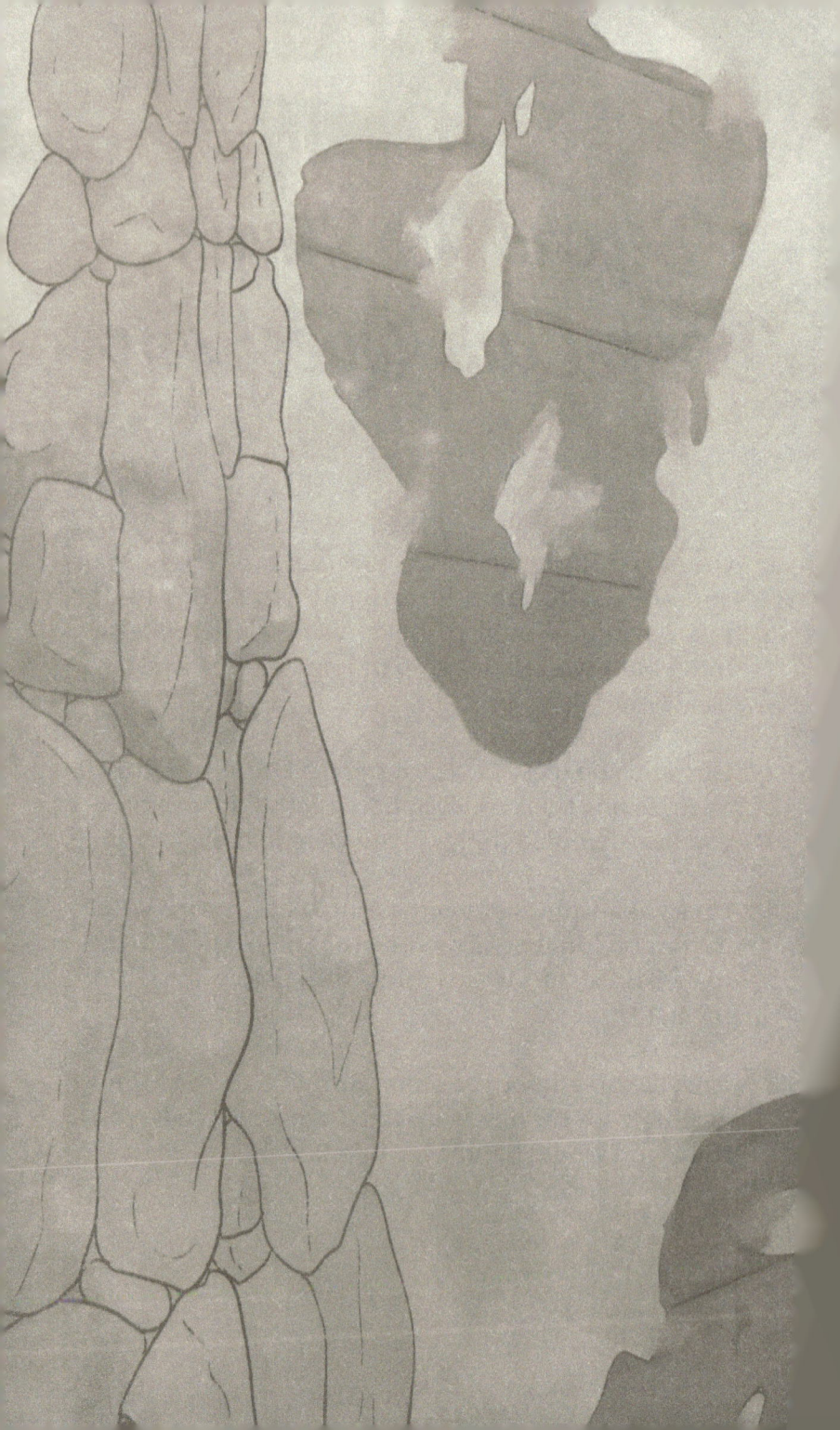

Author Bio

Dominic N. Ashen is an award-winning author and avid reader, with a focus on gay, BDSM-themed erotica. After spending his youth in search of books with characters who were more like himself - queer ones, specifically - he decided to start creating some of his own. His first book, Steel & Thunder, was published in 2021, and was named a Distinguished Favorite in the 2021 NYC Big Book Awards. His stories star queer protagonists, most often gay and bisexual men, and feature themes of dominance, submission, and all sorts of kinks. Dominic loves the fantasy, sci-fi, and horror genres, with a penchant for writing longer stories where he is able to weave in the sex and kink right alongside the plot.

Website: https://www.dominicashen.com/
Patreon: https://www.patreon.com/dominicashen
Twitter: https://twitter.com/DomNAshen
Facebook: https://www.facebook.com/dom.n.ashen
Instagram: https://www.instagram.com/dom.n.ashen

More books from
4 Horsemen Publications

LGBT Erotica

Dominic N. Ashen
Steel & Thunder
Storms & Sacrifice
Secrets & Spires
Arenas & Monsters
My Three Orc Dads: a Novella
Before the Storm: a Novella

Eskay Kabba
Hidden Love
Not So Hidden
Signs of Affection
Deeply Devoted to Him
Honest Love
A Plane and Simple Connection

Grayson Ace
How I Got Here
First Year Out of the Closet
You're Only a Top?
You're Only a Bottom?
I Think I'm a Serial Swiper

Lookin in All the Wrong Places
What Makes Me a Whore?
A Breach in Confidentiality
Back Door Pass
My European Adventure
An Unexpected Affair
Finding True Love
The Dr. Cage Chronicles

Leo Sparx
Before Alexander
Claiming Alexander
Taming Alexander
Saving Alexander
The Fall of the House of Otter
The Case of Armando

Robert Lewis
Someone to Love
Someone to Come Home To
Someone to Kiss

LGBT Romance

AJ Buchannan
Orchestrated Love

Eskay Kabba
Hidden Love
Not So Hidden
Signs of Affection
Deeply Devoted to Him
Honest Love
A Plane and Simple Connection

Lucas LaMont
Roman's Reckoning: Type 6
Mikaél's Moment: Type 6
Stephan's Resurgence: Type 5
Anastasia's Arrival: Type 6

Stormie Skyes
Check Yes, No, or Maybe

V.C. Willis
The Prince's Priest
The Priest's Assassin
The Assassin's Saint
The Champion's Lord

Discover more at
4HorsemenPublications.com